is the author of s Rice, a Detective Sergeant with Lothian and Borders Police. Alexander McCall Smith said of *Blood in the Water*, the first book in the series: 'There is not a dull page from start to finish'. The other titles in the series are *Where the Shadow Falls*, *Dying of the Light*, *No Sorrow to Die*, *The Road to Hell* and *Troubled Waters*. *Blood in the Water* and *Troubled Waters* were among the most borrowed eBooks in UK libraries in 2020.

She also began a new crime series with *The Good Priest*, featuring Father Vincent Ross, a priest who through intelligence, combined with an ear for gossip, manages to solve crimes. The second in the Father Vincent Ross series is on its way. Her most recent book is *The End of the Line*, an unusual crime novel chosen by the *Sunday Times* Crime Club as one of the best crime novels to take on holiday in 2019.

Prior to taking up writing, Gillian worked for a time as an agony aunt in teenagers' magazines and then, for many years, as an Advocate at the Scottish Bar specialising in medical negligence and agricultural law cases. The majority of her work was in Civil Law but she also conducted a number of criminal trials in the High Court of Justiciary. She lives in the country with her husband and daughter plus assorted cats, dogs, hens and geese.

Other books by Gillian Galbraith:

*Blood in the Water*
*Where the Shadow Falls*
*Dying of the Light*
*No Sorrow to Die*
*The Road to Hell*
*Troubled Waters*
*The Good Priest*
*The End of the Line*

# LOVE
# LIES
# BLEEDING

# LOVE LIES BLEEDING

GILLIAN GALBRAITH

FinnStar
Books

First published in 2021 by FinnStar Books
The Old School House
9 Station Road
Roslin
EH25 9LP



ISBN: 978-1-9989962-0-9
eBook ISBN: 978-1-9989962-1-6



*British Library Cataloguing-in-Publication Data*
A catalogue record for this book is available from the British Library.



Set in Italian Garamond BT by
Tom Johnstone Editorial Services

Printed and bound in Great Britain
by Bell & Bain Ltd., Glasgow

## Acknowledgements

Douglas Edington
Daisy Galbraith
Robert Galbraith

## Dedication

To Alison, violinist and fishing friend

# I
# 2021

While I await my deliverance, I have something to say; something important, something about love.

Though still a man, I no longer possess a soul. Yesterday, it fled the crumbling shell that used to house it; feeling only a tingle of relief, I suspect, on leaving such an ancient unsavoury retreat, the plumbing now failing, moths multiplying in the fabrics and the electrics long since blown. Fey I am not, but, if you can believe it, I sensed my soul's exit; felt myself an ounce lighter, my breath shallower, my heartbeat weaker. As it flew upwards, a breeze ruffled the few wisps of white hair loyal enough to continue to cling to my freckled scalp.

If I am strictly truthful, the inadequacy of my soul's abode may not have been the only reason for its flight from my person. Rats, apparently, leave sinking ships and this ninety-seven-year-old vessel has a gaping hole in its barnacled bows, fathoms below the water line. Am I dying? All I know is that the hole is large enough for sharks and rays to swim through, without as much as a sandpapery tail or fin touching the timbers, and a giant squid might even squeeze herself through such an inviting opening – a baby one, anyway.

My heart is failing me.

Immobile in my adjustable hospital bed, my legs made of lead, I must concentrate. A male nurse, smiling at me in that uneasy way that betrays kindness but also wariness, adjusts the cage above my swollen feet.

'Would you like a shower this morning, Jock?' he asks.

'I do need one,' I reply, (and I chose the word with care) though fearful at the thought of the impending ablutions.

But this is not a story about me. It is about love, an otherworldly, sublime love, and about Laura. But already I am getting ahead of myself; to be frank, it is difficult not to hurry onwards when one's next breath may, literally, be one's last. Does that mayfly lifespan trouble me? No, frankly, not a jot. Well, perhaps bravado has got the better of me in that boast, but I am far more afraid of the more imminent horror, of being lifted in the Invacare Birdie hoist for my thrice weekly sluicing, than of reaching my final destination. Wherever that may be.

In my tomb of scarcely living flesh, one part of me remains free, free and intact. My mind. Usually it ignores the present or, unsurprisingly, treats it with disdain as unworthy of its attention. Why would it not? My todays extend like vast featureless plains, the colour of ash, or porridge, in all their drab flatness to the end of my horizon. Truthfully, for years, the presence of a bluetit on the birdfeeder at my window has counted as a red-letter day. Equally, conscious of having no future, my mind spends its time roaming in the past, soaring between my nursery and the robing room of the law courts, inhaling the scent of white jasmine or a sweet Philadelphus, making love with Laura in a Mediterranean bay, walking through the Meadows on a sunlit morning and, generally, enjoying itself in that large but lost world.

I visualise my memory as a condor, gliding on thermals, warm winds under its vast wings, supporting it as it spirals upwards, surveying its domain thousands of feet below. From on high, some features are too small, too blurred, too difficult to make out, but one more lazy-winged circle, a few hundred feet lower, and everything can be seen with perfect clarity. Then my past is as bright as a peacock's tail. And part of that past, the part that I return to time after time, holds Laura.

I met her, if you can call it that, in inauspicious circumstances. In a courtroom. She was dressed in a black suit with a high-collared white blouse, crisp as a waitress. In my role as a judge, I had been allocated a couple of undefended divorces and was napping my way through the second of them, (having accidentally slipped a Mogadon into my mouth in the belief that it was a heartburn pill), when the slender woman in the witness box, Laura, began to speak.

I had never heard a voice like hers. Low, burnt umber in colour and as reassuring, as warm, rich and comforting, as molasses. I straightened my wig and sat up, compelled to make her notice me.

'Mrs Ellis,' I said, having taken a quick glance at the papers and seen Ellis v. Ellis on the Closed Record, 'did you say that your husband was a gynaecologist or was it a urologist?'

From the back of the court, a fellow released a mirthless laugh.

'No, my Lord,' she replied, looking up at me from the witness box, 'I said a geologist.'

I nodded sagely, apparently doing my job in the dispassionate manner expected of the judiciary. But, inside, I sensed that everything had changed. Love, that brightest of bright lights, flooded my being. Low, lush cello music started up in my head, almost reducing me to tears. I felt warm, alive and suddenly exquisitely sensitive to the world and everything in it. Transported. I could not take my eyes off her.

What is love? Two of my nurses, whilst slapping ointment on my bedsores, occasionally share their 'emotional issues' with me. Experience has taught them to expect no answer if they use the expression 'partner', as my reaction, a coughing fit, immediately obliterates their quasi- confidences. The very word functions as an expectorant. I cannot abide it, with its connotations of firms, accounts and ledgers. Lover, surely! Mine must have been a love of a different order, one that could go by no other name, and I say that as a man once easily impressed by, susceptible to, the charms of the opposite sex. Can those who have never inhaled the scent of an English rose, heady as Rosa 'Munstead Wood', imagine it? Can the blessed, those who have, describe it to those who have lacked a sense of smell from birth? No, and that is not arrogance, that is a straightforward fact.

My own life divides into BL and AL. Before Laura and After Laura. Before her, I was not truly alive, not truly myself, because my best self, the one I was meant to be, had never emerged. It is embarrassing to admit it, but in this romantic tale, I did not resemble

Tolstoy's suave Count Vronsky; a man easily amused, in control, sophisticated when in search of entertainment and, finally, exasperated by his lover. No, I was (an unusually large-nosed) version of Anna Karenina. You see, the more loving one was me, always me, but I am too decrepit nowadays to stagger off, unlike Mrs Karenin, in search of a merciful locomotive. I had my chance to do so earlier. Actually, for a decade or so, a wine gum going down the wrong way has been a more likely means of deliverance from my plight, if a little less picturesque and, arguably, lacking that . . . that . . . what? Epic quality?

# 2
# 1975 and onwards

I was obsessed. I pursued Laura, hunted her down as a hound might a hare. Rightly or wrongly, I have always considered intelligence (mine and that in others) invaluable. Excessive veneration of brains is the number one vice of the legal profession, and I was not immune to it. Should you doubt it, I will admit something I once believed; that if one of those star-struck Magi had, say, tumbled off his camel and a Q.C. had been required to bring gifts in his stead, some IQ enhancing drug would have been thrust upon the babe instead of presents of gold, frankincense or myrrh. Because 'Hey Presto!' if Christ had been cleverer, that duo of thieves, stretched on their Golgotha gallows, would have had to chat amongst themselves. Veronica's facecloth would still be by the soap, Judas would have had to find another cheek to kiss. But Christ would still have risen.

Overblown fancy, you think? I overegg the pudding? Granted. Few nonagenarians are strangers to hyperbole; we haven't the time for moderation, nuance, subtlety. The point is that by pinpointing her haunts, her interests, her friends, I succeeded, after a couple of months, somehow, in enchanting her. I used my only asset; my brain.

The court papers gave me a few clues, including her address. The Closed Record stated: 'The defender called the pursuer a "bloodsucker" and "leech" then hit the pursuer on the head when she returned from her life drawing class.' The brute!

How many such classes could there be in Edinburgh? A lot as it turned out. Morningside, Blackhall, the High Street, Stockbridge and all points east, south, west and north. Finally, in desperation, I tailed her from her home through the winding streets to her class in Howe Street; then, the following week, I joined it. In that dusty church hall, I whiled away my time, trusty HB motionless in my hand, watching her deft fingers draw whilst agonising over the thought that the male model's naked endowments might arouse unrealistic expectations. A preening airhead, I had no doubt.

Opening a window to let in enough cold draught to transform the saveloy into a chipolata, I listened in to every conversation. Pierre, the drawing master, asked his students for suggestions for the background music, and Mrs Ellis (or Laura as I now knew her in my own head) volunteered Bach, Handel and Corelli, out of the hundreds of CDs available, and hummed along to the Brandenburg Concerto once it was playing. So, I got tickets for the Queen's Hall, the Assembly Rooms, the Usher Hall, wherever anyone played anything by any of them. A few weeks later, in one of the bars in the Usher Hall, I sidled up to her, gin and tonic in hand, to discuss the extraordinary coincidence of our meeting, and my own fondness for, would you believe it, Bach.

You get the picture. Though I say it myself, I played a blinder, slipping in effortlessly my all but equal affection for Handel, and, yes, Corelli. Left to my own devices, I will confess to you, I preferred Sidney Devine and Glen Campbell on the car stereo (does 'Wichita Linesman' have an equal?), but that meeting was neither the time, nor the place, to mention it. In any event, lovers, all lovers, lie, mould themselves around the outline of the beloved. One woman, her interest doubtless piqued by my judicial title, looked me in the eye and claimed Burn Murdoch on Interdict was 'the most interesting book she had ever read'. I, temporarily besotted by a slim Italian I had been introduced to, tasted and swallowed calamari, declaring it 'delicious'. But no cephalopod's limb has wrapped itself around my tongue since. Thinking of it now, I gag.

Learning from Nina, an aged, paint-spattered Scandinavian with whom I became acquainted at the Drawing Class, that Laura adored the Argentinian tango I determined to learn the dance myself. Once mastered, I planned to surprise her, literally sweep her off her feet. However, after one lesson I had to abandon ship. 'You have absolutely no sense of time!' my partner, Mercedes, hissed angrily into my groin, that being as near an approximation of the chest-to-chest clasp our respective heights would allow. This was not a revelation to me. By then we had only been dancing (I use the word loosely; lurching would be more accurate) for about three minutes. Thinking of Laura, I attempted to marshal my oversized feet into a parallel walk but, somehow, left one behind which elicited a 'Shit!' from Mercedes as she endeavoured not to spike me with her red stiletto. The end came when, striving to perform a figure, I asked her for how much longer the class went on. Murmuring another 'Shit!' she left me stranded alone on the floor, and I learnt from a charitable fellow pupil that conversation whilst dancing the tango is forbidden. The teacher, a male, offered to partner me, which I much appreciated, but I retreated, unable to thole further humiliation. Or to dance.

When she heard of my fiasco, Laura awarded me marks for effort and, slightly shyly and to my delight, circled with me whilst humming an accompaniment, until laughing she said, 'Unhand me, Lord Hand. I don't think you can have a drop of Latin blood in your body.'

'And you do?' I teased, the naturalness of her movement having made, to my mind, such a question rhetorical.

'A drop or two . . . a little French, some Albanian, Argentinian, Romanian, Polish . . . the list goes on.'

Despite the minuscule odds in my favour, I persisted. You see, nature had not favoured me with good looks. In my teenage years, testosterone having conspired against me to disfigure my previously acceptable self, it hurt to see photographs of my former incarnations at the age of two, five, seven or whatever on my mother's dressing table. In pride of place. Who wants their irretrievable past flung, like a bucket of blood, in their face? My adolescent appearance offended my mother, a woman in thrall to her own eyes. How could a dazzler like her produce something as 'plain' (to put it politely) as me? She seemed to believe in parthenogenic reproduction, as my short-lived father's looks did not seem to come into the equation. But it went far beyond my plainness. In her mind, virtue and beauty went hand in hand, and the converse was equally true. Thus, my ugliness was judged to be not purely skin deep. In her prime, my mother resembled the notorious but glamorous Margaret, Duchess of Argyll, a socialite whose romantic escapades ended in both scandal and the Divorce Courts. Mama informed me that 'poor sweet Margaret was crucified by that hideous Lord Wheatley and his unsightly legal cronies'.

Sometimes, in a rather naïve, childish way, I struggled against her doctrine. But I could never win, as hers was not a mind susceptible to rational argument. 'So, Marilyn Monroe was a saint, I suppose?' I said, once, stung by her unconcealed anxiety that some friend of hers should meet me.

'Your father certainly thought she was a heavenly body,' she replied solemnly, taking a sip of sherry, quite satisfied that the point was hers.

'And Winston Churchill, I suppose he was some sort of devil?'

'Oh, Jock,' she replied, defending her position with ease, 'he was a very, very good-looking young man!'

'And did his soul blacken as he began to melt, disintegrate, developing a moon face, the jowls of a bulldog and six chins?' I persisted.

'No, no, everyone ages . . . even the good. But beauty shapes you, determines how you look at the world and how it looks at you.'

'How does the world look at me?'

'It doesn't,' she said, 'it covers its eyes!' With those words, she released a tinkling laugh, ushering me away at the sound of a car arriving and crunching on gravel.

I retired in my short trousers, bruised and defeated.

So, no photographs of my teenage self ever found themselves by her ivory hairbrushes, although the photogenic toddlers that were kept there were, to all effects, as good as dead. Those snaps were now of pretty phantoms, non-existent beings and as meaningful, or meaningless, as any ripped in a random fashion from Hello or someone else's family albums. To work off my chagrin, I used to stalk around her chintz dressing table, accidently knocking the images of my rivals for her love to the floor, or stealthily removing those I found most offensive.

In fact, there was no place within our cold townhouse for photos of my spotty self, my ill-proportioned body, although that was me, the real me. The me of the moment, the only extant me but, self-evidently, the unacceptable me. Ever. Remembering it anew, I confess, I feel a hot, recurring fury possess me. Once I overheard my only parent (since my father had died when I was three) describe me as 'A big disappointment'. Her love, you see, was conditional; and that condition I could not fulfil. But I must try to 'let it go', as counsellors have advised over the years. Grudges against ghosts are fatuous.

Post-puberty, did the ugly duckling turn into a swan? No, into a six-foot-six shoebill, since you ask; but even those most hideous birds find mates and my story, this story, is one of love, although it is, I should make clear, a love that crosses species. My own darling, Laura, was a swan.

My perseverance, no, my love, won her heart and, eventually, her hand. Of course, I have not described my beloved, and I could let you imagine her yourself, but whoever you might conjure up, it would not be her, and, no offence intended, but is your imagination up to the task? Mine certainly was not. Perhaps, on reflection, all I need say is that she had the clearest blue eyes in the world. Eyes that draw you in, embrace you, shelter you. Eyes that can only be trusted. Innocent eyes. And, the other thing to remember, is that she was a swan. Oh yes, one further detail. As a snaggle-toothed creature, I was thrilled to notice her own crooked eye teeth and how fetching they were. Wolfishly sexy, some might say. She was as dark, deep and alluring as the night, and I was powerless, possessed. I gave myself up to her.

By then, I was past my own short-lived prime, although (now I think about it) still startlingly handsome by my current standard. Everything being, of course, relative. Nowadays, to picture my face, think the lovechild of Klaus Kinski and Tenniel's Duchess from Alice's Adventures in Wonderland. Then starve the offspring and cure it as one would an Arbroath smokie. Voila! A yellowing, wrinkled skull. Me.

But, at that stage, embarking on the adventure of my sixth decade, I still had spare flesh, had not yet begun to shrink and sported naturally bouffant grey hair with a middle parting, such as is now our monarch's favoured style. 'Prosperous' is how others described me in the 1970s (a euphuism for fat) due, I admit, in part to too many bread-and-butter puddings at the New Club. I was a man of substance, literally and metaphorically. The mirror in my robing room reflected me in my red judicial robes as a sweaty, irritable Father Christmas, one far too beefy to chance any chimneys other than those belonging to a power station. But, though eighteen years my junior, Laura seemed to see something in her fat shoebill, someone she could love.

On the night we became engaged, I took her to the Café Royal. Over dinner in its tiled splendour I fiddled incessantly with the ring case on my lap like love-struck boy. Fear of rejection meant that most of my lobster bisque went back with the plates, for once, and made my heart pound like a steam-hammer against my ribs. Pudding over, and on the edge of losing my nerve, I said weakly, 'Today is my fifty-first birthday, I hope I am not too old for you?'

'Age,' she replied, 'means nothing to me.'

I believed her. And, fumblingly, I proffered her my mother's ruby and diamond ring.

'Will you m . . . m . . . marry me?'

As you may imagine, I had not stammered when I had practised that in front of the mirror, in the car on the way to the restaurant and in the Gents at the place. In fact, I had not stammered for over thirty-five years.

'Yes.'

Hearing the word, tears came to my eyes, but I manufactured a sneeze and caught them whilst dabbing my monstrous beak with my hankie. If I had died that night, it would have been as a happy man.

Our nest was in the New Town of Edinburgh, a whole, three-storey house in an elegant square with a garden in the centre. Forgive me, but old habits die hard. The memory of threats to disembowel me by Glasgow drug barons (stale as they now are) prevent me from providing our actual location, but suffice to say, Laura was thrilled with our Georgian fastness. Before she moved in the place was furnished as I imagine an upmarket undertaker's premises might be – tasteful, corporate, soothing and completely impersonal. Of course, my study was not littered with pamphlets describing how the ashes of a loved one could be transformed into a brooch or bejewelled kilt pin (for Him) but, apart from that, the bereaved, through their haze of tears, would have recognised the ambience. Throughout my time as a QC I had held many of my consultations in the drawing room there and, for some reason, had felt that any display of my private life might undermine my authority. I was, when I think about it now, a little repressed, a little tight-arsed, some might say. (Nowadays, swaddled in nappies and a slave to Immodium, I wish I could be more tight-arsed.)

Laura changed everything, and to my delight she loved spending money on our home. Burgundy silk cushions appeared, photos in leather frames, velvet curtains, tasselled chair covers, rich flock wallpapers. Scents of sandalwood, stephanotis and bergamot took the place of Imperial Leather. Most importantly, photographs of me appeared everywhere. Sumptuous is the word that comes to mind to describe her taste, and I revelled in it. It had nothing safe, respectable or timid about it and made no apology for its magnificence, or its almost gothic quality. Blood-red was her colour. One icy evening, returning from Parliament Square after a long arduous hearing on, imagine it, Rights of Way, I walked into my house and felt I had ascended to

Heaven. The Wolf Glen scene from Weber's Der Freischutz hit my ears, the scent of the lilies in the nearby vase mixed with a hint of roast beef drifted up my nose and a wave of warmth bathed my numb cheeks. Unseen, tears of joy came to my eyes. I felt that I had, at last, found what the fortunate find long before they reach their half-century. Love, warmth, domesticity, call it any or all of those things. All I knew was that my old companion, loneliness, had been banished and I had, in the fullest sense, arrived.

Looking at my beloved as she raised a forkful of blood-dripping beef to her mouth, I found it hard to believe my good fortune. The only light in the room came from the candles in the candelabra, their light catching the diamonds dangling from her ears and throwing deep shadows around her features and making her cheekbones sharper than ever. I do not paint but that night, looking at the scene, I longed to do justice to it. To her.

At lunchtime the next day I went to Hamilton and Inches, a shop previously as unfamiliar to me as one selling saucy lingerie, and perused their jewellery counter. A lady, clad entirely in black, set an array of glittering rings before my eyes.

'Lovely,' I said, 'but have you anything special, really unique?'

Whispering, as one might in a church, that she knew of something that might fit the bill, she waddled towards an open doorway.

My Crombie coat, never mind my high colour and sponge-bag trousers, had reassured her that I was not a time-waster and, humming to herself, she returned from the back quarters with a necklace of tiny, polished bloodstones and pearls with a platinum catch. A miniature horse, composed of diamonds, dangled from it. Wordlessly, she placed it on the glass counter.

'Modern,' she said, adding when I said nothing, 'made by the jeweller, Paul D'Eath of Rheims, but very collectible, very sought after.'

'You think she'd like it?'

'It certainly should fit most ladies' bill, sir,' she replied.

I fingered it, gasped at the price and then bought it. Laura adored horses.

All afternoon, as Sidney Dunlop QC imagined he was sharing the finer points of Auctor in Rem Suam with me, my mind returned to my precious and how best to surprise her, thrill her with my tribute. Should I rush in and hand over the beribboned box to her immediately? Make clues for her to solve that would lead her to it? Or should I wait till we got into bed, place the cold stones around her slender neck, then shine a torch on it, and set it to sparkle? Embed it in a bar of the finest French soap? How to maximise her delight? Even then I had an inkling of a truth about myself: wise old judge as I might be, my inexperience in love had left me stunted, childlike; a deficiency I attempted to hide. I settled on concealing the necklace amongst some handmade chocolates, each one individually wrapped in red and gold paper. Chancing upon it in the bonbons, after only two eaten, she threw her arms around me and gave me a deep, heartfelt kiss. That night we made love and afterwards I lay, exhausted, in her cool white arms. I am not a religious man, but leaning against her, my head on her breast, I thanked the Lord for my existence and for making her love me. Remarkably, as my soul magnified the Lord, she stirred and let out a sweet little moan. I swallowed my usual Mogadon and, thinking of her and nothing but her, sailed off to sleep.

The next day, although I felt strangely drained by my own ardour, I walked to Parliament House with a spring in my step. My judicial colleague, Evan Palmer, caught up with me as I wended my way up the Mound, tapping me on the shoulder as I passed the turn off to Market Street. We carried on side by side. Planning had been his forte, a subject I hope to die in ignorance of. His real specialty was wives, and he had had four of his own. Three, I believe, supported by extensions to the M8 motorway and one by an Asda megastore. The most recent had been a fellow member's wife; a sin akin to cannibalism.

'You, old boy,' he said, 'look like a cat that has been at the cream.'

'Only the crème de la crème for this Tom,' I said, fatuously, feeling as if I had, inadvertently, turned myself into the personification of a Donald McGill seaside postcard, and appalled at my own transformation of Laura into a sandy-bosomed cartoon companion. Unaware of my self-induced consternation, he continued, 'You're a different man since you married. To be frank, Jock, I thought you'd missed the bus, would die as a confirmed, old bachelor. Not that there's anything wrong with that, of course. How is the beautiful Lady Hand? We must have you round to dinner sometime soon; Ellen is very keen to meet her.'

Ellen, my arse! Slightly breathless because of the steepness of the hill, I nodded and then steered our conversation towards the forthcoming election for Clerk of the Faculty of Advocates, hinting that my money was on Palmer's own son, Malcolm. He took the bait, and I kept to myself that I'd as likely back a crippled Kiang in the Grand National. I had no intention of introducing Laura to a Casanova like him; it would be like introducing a goldfish to a cat. I looked my age, but that bugger, on his diet of young female flesh, has always passed for someone a good ten years younger than me though he is, in fact (chronologically only), my twin. Sessions of squash? Weights in the attic? Some wonder gene? Who knows? Planning may be dull but, somehow, he had ensnared the past and present Lady Palmers with the poetry of development plans, planning circulars, stop notices and so on. Thinking about it, if my own spin on ecclesiastical law had captivated my beloved, planning law could well have some musky appeal for the fairer sex, for all I knew.

From my elevated perch in Court 10, I dreamt the day away, half an ear on Dunlop's submissions and somehow, somehow the hours passed. My judicial role, like tarnished silver, had lost its lustre for me. Once I would have sold my soul to be able to flick an end of my long-bottomed wig at the populace as I marched from the Courts to St Giles, robes billowing like a bat's wings, in the annual kirking. Now, its only value to me was that with it came a title: Lord Hand of Ellery. An offering that I could lay at Laura's delicate, blue-veined feet, bestow it upon her, bedeck her in furs and, in the minds of the masses, ennoble her.

Against the unwelcome background hum of passages from the Local Government (Scotland) Act 1894 being recited in Dunlop's nasal tones, I ruminated over more important matters; to wit – the nature and effect of love. For me, when my beloved was not present, it was as if all light had gone from the world, or every vestige of colour had been drained from it. All my joy, all warmth, everything fine and good emanated from her, depended upon her. She was my sun. I felt like a mole which had spent a lifetime underground, only to pop up through its hill and perceive, for the first time and thanks to her, the world and all the glories with which it was blessed.

With her, for the first time in my life, I had explored the beauties of my home city at night. One walk, in particular, is etched on my memory. Moonlight, she loved; lighting that accentuated shadows, sharpened outlines and transformed the mundane into the mysterious. One icy, moonlit evening we met on the Esplanade and set off walking, hand in hand, along the cobbled street that leads down from the Castle, wove in and out of Old Fishmarket Close, Advocates Close, Carrubber's close and few more of the courtyards and wynds that stem from the Royal Mile like the branches of a fir tree. In Anchor Close there was an auld body sitting against the wall, skirts on the ground, hems drawing up the pool of urine around her. As I approached, she held out her nut-brown hand for pennies and, fishing in my overcoat, I found a note and gave it to her. The stench of beer hit my nostrils, though whether from the vagrant, Annie, or the nearby breweries, I could not tell.

'You, Jock Hand, are a good man,' Laura said later, placing a kiss on my cold cheek.

'Oh, I've known Annie for years . . . she used to be a policewoman,' I replied, starting down the steps for Cockburn Street.

'You accept people for what they are.'

'I try.'

You accept me,' she said laughing, linking her arm in mine. I inhaled the scent of roses.

'With both hands,' I replied in the same spirit, marvelling at her inverted view of things. It was she who accepted me. I was the cat. She was the King.

At her request, our final destination was to be the Greyfriars Kirkyard. The moon bathed the city in its pale, watery light, but with her beside me our meander had never seemed so full of possibilities, so stimulating, so exciting. Owls serenaded us by the Campbell Crypt, and as we looked up there seemed more stars in the sky than ever before. I kissed her.

Yet none of what we saw that night was new to me. After all, my own workplace, Parliament House, sits snug by St Giles and the High Street runs beside it. I had walked those streets, clattered up and down those steps, countless times from the early years of my devilling until my elevation to the bench. But in her company, the town of Burke and Hare, the plague, Deacon Brodie and the blood-spattered Heart of Midlothian became real and alive, and the Signet Library and other dusty institutions that dominated my staid legal existence faded into the background, became as pale and insipid as a badly executed watercolour. Maybe I now saw things through her foreign eyes; an ancient city, one peopled by ghosts, with ravens on the battlements and dark deeds in the wynds. All I know is that seeing such sights entranced her, enlivened her and made the air around us almost electric in its intensity.

I strove to formulate my thoughts about her. But language, or at least the variety of the English language used by me, could not, I decided, adequately express Laura's effect upon me. Maybe the Metaphysical poets might have stood a chance, or Michael Drayton or Rabbie Burns, but not me. Definitely, not me. A mind shaped by such things as the construction of statutes, the analysis of sub-clauses or schedules and the extraction of the Ratio Decidendi from a hundred pages of a densely written judgement is unlikely to have either the vocabulary, or the innate musicality, necessary to do justice to the ineffable beauty, the marvel that is romantic love. Time after time, I returned to the same childish mantra found hacked by the penknives of the illiterate on every second urban tree: 'I love Laura'. I could do no better.

Although, as if it made any difference, in my head I altered the emphasis with each declaration: I love Laura; I LOVE Laura; I love LAURA.

Meanwhile in the background Dunlop droned on, declaring that he was 'Moving on to a new chapter, entitled the effect of Rhins District Committee of Wigtownshire County Council V Cuninghame on the Renfrew case.'

I released a long- suppressed yawn, and, doing so, felt a sudden, unexpected cold shiver of fear. What had come over me? Once, such fancy footwork as he was executing on the head of a pin had fascinated me, had been my life, my whole existence. Truly, my raison d'etre. What other had I had? By rights, my ears ought to be pricked; my juices running. I should have been gripped by the cleverness of the fellow's argument, intrigued by his exploration of a new legal point, eager for him to lead me, hand in hand, to our new enlightenment.

But something, no, everything had changed. The subterranean creature had become intoxicated, bewitched, addicted to the blue of the sky, the stars, the song of the birds. He could not contemplate a return to his previous dark, damp life regardless of the predators or other club-footed fiends now alive to his existence. I could not go back into the dark. I had become, I realised, dependent upon Laura, and that realization, for a passing second, frightened me.

# 3

A couple of months later, I rolled down Frederick Street having, yet again, overindulged myself in the New Club and arrived, lilies in hand, at my own doorstep.

Laura seemed a little subdued at supper, low enough for me to detect her mood despite my alcohol-blunted mind. I had been aware of such dips in her spirit, increasingly over the last week. She was playing with her food, moving it around the plate but rarely putting her spoon to her mouth. Her Beaumes-de-Venise was untouched. Catching a glimpse in the mirror of the reddened turnip that then passed for my face, my fat fingers encircling a wine glass, and looking across at her pale loveliness, I suddenly was reminded of Beauty and the Beast. No doubt others, seeing us, had thought the same before, but for me, it was a soul-destroying revelation. The Queen of Puddings turned to dust in my mouth and my appetite disappeared in that instant. How had I missed the blindingly obvious until then? What did I have to offer other than my wealth and my judicial title? And Midas, as things turned out (certainly according to that talented lesbian poet who versified the myth), had not proved much of a catch.

She would break the news kindly. She must have met someone, fallen helplessly in love. Of course! Before I had felt the power of romantic love, I had told myself that I would never keep a caged bird as a pet or companion. For, if the canary flapped its wings only once against the bars of the golden cage, I would have to open the door and watch the bird spread its wings and fly off into freedom, into the wide cloudless sky. I would lose something I loved. If the creature was to remain, it must want my company every bit as much as I wanted its company. Actually, anxious that I was witnessing just such a phenomenon, the first flap, I felt physically sick. I could not open the cage door, could not even contemplate it. I could not lose her.

Mentally, I added another golden lock to the cage door.

'Darling,' she began, and I consciously steeled myself for whatever might follow, flinching, readying myself to receive the blow. Already my insides had turned to liquid. She was far too good for the likes of me.

'Yes?'

'I went to the doctor today . . .'

In my panic, the blood must have left my face, because she pushed back her chair and came to me, putting both hands on my cheeks. Cancer, it must be cancer.

'It's alright, Jock, it's alright. I am alright. There is nothing wrong with me.'

'Then why did you go to the doctor?' In my terror, my voice sounded high as a castrato.

'Because I'm expecting a baby. I had been feeling a little sick, off-colour and my sense of smell was becoming troublesomely good. Anything and everything seemed to make me nauseous, but before speaking to you, telling you, I wanted to be one hundred percent certain.'

'What, what did you say?'

'We are having a baby'

'We are having a baby?'

'Yes.'

'We are having a baby?'

'That's what I said, yes. WE ARE HAVING A BABY!'

Words had never failed me before. After all, I was a professional rhetorician, not a parrot. My eloquence had ensured my smooth and speedy passage from lowly white wig to QC to a full-blown (I did, by then, have a certain pneumatic quality) Senator of the College of Justice. But, rendered speechless by her news, I put my arms around her, relieved, a new, overpowering happiness filling my being. Laura was well. And pregnant. And all my adult life, I had wanted a child, boy or girl. Joy overwhelmed me, reduced me to a smiling mute.

In my years in the wilderness, my solitary years, I had never confided such a wish to anyone, thinking it would sound pathetic, and, as I got older a little creepy conceivably. Women of childbearing age who have such aspirations are thought normal; a question hangs over middle-aged men, especially if they are unattractive bachelors, and I, you will recall, resemble a shoebill. In short, in getting such news my cup overflowed with happiness, one of my dearest wishes was about to be fulfilled. I would have a child to dandle on my knee, a stocking to fill at Christmas, and that new-born being, most wonderfully of all, would be our child. Someone else to cherish; our flesh and our blood. We would become a family and, for all time, that infant would tie us together with threads of gold. And I would love my child, whatever it looked like.

'Are you pleased?' she asked, sounding, in the silence, a little unsure.

Where was I to begin? It seemed easier to confess all. At the end of my heartfelt outpouring, it finally occurred to me to ask her if she was pleased. We had, after all, not been married long and had never, odd as it now seems, discussed parenthood.

'I've longed for a child forever, Jock. And now our line, the Hand line, will continue down the centuries! Think of that! But now, right now, my only longing is for a piece of stilton . . . but it's all gone. Except for the bit on your plate.'

'All that I have is yours, my love,' I said, moving it towards her with my knife.

In between adjudicating on interminable motion rolls, debates and proofs, plus, I suppose, producing the odd written judgment, I haunted Jenners, Forsyths and other such 'bedroom' emporia willingly. I had a nursery to furnish. You have to remember such domesticity was, for me, a novelty, an unexplored land, and I got a strange enjoyment out of appearing relatively normal. I nearly boxed the ears of an over-familiar assistant in Binns who referred to Laura as 'Mum' and me as 'the happy Grandpa'. Seeing my rising colour, Laura linked her arm close in mine and gave me a saucy wink such as would be unlikely to be exchanged between those of the forbidden degrees. The boy quailed.

When I was sent away on High Court circuits to far-away exotic places such as Inverness or Aberdeen, even Glasgow, I resented the time taken and indulged in no post-circuit celebrations, telephoning at length and speeding back to Auld Reekie and my beloved in my battered Rover at the first opportunity. People noticed. Jim Gallagher, my friend and the then Lord President, took me to one side in the Library and, with genuine concern on his face, asked me why I had turned down the Bar and Bench Golf match.

'You always play. We're a bit worried about you. We never see you about Parliament House other than in one or other of the courts, nowadays you scurry off home. Come along to Muirfield, it promises to be a good day out, a good match?'

It was a kind inquiry; my ability at swinging a golf club would rival Kylie Minogue's skill at tossing the caber. Most of my fellow judges belonged to the Honourable Company of Edinburgh Golfers and were competitive by disposition, and my inclusion, as they knew only too well, guaranteed only that sand would sully the floor of the golf buggy. And that we would lose to the Bar.

In the old days, my final putt having bounced off a flagpole again or dribbled into a drain, I would return, a smidgen intoxicated, along the sinuous coast road to my tasteful, tidy undertaker's parlour and my cold single bed, assuring myself that I would not let my colleagues, or myself, down ever again. After one cup of black coffee in the kitchen, my cheeks would burn as I recreated in my mind's eye my bathetic air-shots at the 12th and the inconsiderate burn that got in the way at the 14th. At least, I would console myself, I had not succumbed to the urge to cheat, overpowering as it had been on multiple occasions. One year, having thrashed furiously and fruitlessly in a bunker for too long, I had flung the ball out. Passing me, the oily presence that was then the Lord Justice Clerk hissed, 'Well, well, Lord Hand . . . of God'. He went on his way smirking, the turd.

In fact, the only Bar social event that I attended that year was the Faculty Ball. We went in a party of six, Palmer fortuitously absent on a Commission in Rome, and, for once, I was on the dancefloor throughout. As you may know, the toes of the shoebill are exceptionally long, but I managed to cram mine into some patent pumps and shuffle about on the dancefloor with the worst of them. Part of the reason, I admit, for my uncustomary reeling (a rowdy Hamilton House once brought on palpitations) was to ensure that no other partner ingratiated himself with my beloved. Duke of Perth, darling? We really must! An Eightsome? One of my favourites! I had thought, wrongly as it turned out, that Laura might sit out quite a few of the dances due to her condition. Instead, she flew, light-footed as a faery, feet hardly touching the ground, weaving her way in and out of the lines as smooth as a ribbon. Sporran and sweat flying about me, in contrast, I reassured myself, arm-in-arm with her, that swans mated for life, were unusually faithful creatures. But doubt slithered in, whispering: 'Swan and swan; but swan and shoebill?'

The trouble was that her beauty was such, so exceptional, that I found myself torn in two. Like some kind of mad Eastern potentate, I had wanted to show her off, flaunt my treasure, yet somehow, not engender any desire to possess or steal my treasure in the breasts of others. The cannibal hordes. Who would not 'scurry' home, with Laura to come back to? Her condition still hardly visible in her black ball gown and long white gloves, she outshone the stars. Truly.

Derek Fleming, uncouth Sheriff of Lanark, cummerbund halfway down his hips and eyes bleary with drink, barked at me in her presence, 'How did you do it, Jocky?'

Saying what others must have thought. I did not dignify the question with an answer. Exhaling a beery gust, the ape turned on his pigeon toes and, though partnerless, immediately managed to weave himself into the nearest line for Strip the Willow, then birl a fat matron so fast that on release she careered, still spinning like a top, into her neighbour. While the Dean's wife was still scooping herself off the ground, glaring at her innocent assailant, Laura and I glided through Parliament Hall, hand in hand, eager to feel the cold night air on our faces. Walking through Princes Street Gardens, moonlight glinting off the rime-covered trees, I broached the subject with my love. 'How did I do it?' I asked, and the inquiry was genuine.

'Only,' she said, 'someone as loveable as you could ask such a question.'

Usually, such an answer would have been comfort enough, but having observed so many eyes fixed on her, I needed more. 'But how, darling, really?'

'Because I love you.'

'But why? You could have any man you wanted.'

Such clumsy persistence made me uneasy, but like a child, I craved her reassurance.

'Because . . .' she said slowly, looking directly at me, 'you are clever, funny, warm, unusually tolerant, generous . . . untidy, thoughtful and incapable of folding a towel.'

'You forgot one thing, missed the crucial one out,' I said, looking pained.

'Many, actually. But what did you have in mind?'

'My unearthly beauty,' I replied, crossing my eyes and shaking my head at her.

'And,' she said, taking my hand again, 'you have the most beautiful soul I know, and, call me odd, but I find shoebills very attractive.'

'And this shoebill, my darling Odd, adores you.'

That night we made love and, later, my hand on her belly, I tried to feel the movement of the child within, the first stirrings of the new life. My reward was one tiny prod to my flattened palm, enough to catch my attention but no more. Somehow, feeling such dainty, fluttering pressure, I knew, with an unshakeable conviction, that our child was a girl. I took my sleeping pill, and with Laura nuzzling herself into her usual position, head beside my head, I began to think of names for my daughter.

Perhaps due to the amount of Faculty champagne I had consumed, the next day I felt unusually weary, but as it was a Saturday, I had planned to do nothing other than a spell of judicial writing. A novel problem, involving a woman who had borne a healthy baby after she had, supposedly, been sterilised, awaited me. Would the subsequent birth of a healthy child entitle the mother to damages, to compensation, for the loss? Thinking of my own dear parent, I had no doubt that she considered herself the loser in hatching a shoebill chick. A cuckoo's egg deposited in her nest would, I feel sure, have been thought a mercy; she would have encouraged the featherless little assassin to rid itself of its brother. In her eighties, shortly before her demise and when her own plumage was a tad threadbare, I tried to reconcile myself with her. Placing a piece of cake on the table in front of her, I put an arm around her emaciated shoulders, readying myself to speak warm words.

'Don't,' she said, feeling no need to elaborate on her own reaction.

No doubt it reflects badly on me, but I did not try twice. Actually, I would give a small fortune to forget the shiver of disgust that rippled through that tiny frame at my touch. Maybe it is a sentimental fantasy on my part, but I believe most sentient creatures are loved by their creators. Even a baby alligator hatching slimily from its egg will make the cold blood of the mugger beside it stir, and the mother rat's spirits gladden at the sight of her naked, blind, offspring. My love for my child will be unconditional, wrapped like a warm cloak around her, protecting her until the last beat of my own heart. Imogen, I will call her. My beloved child.

Reminding myself that the Health Board Judgement was overdue, I began to look over my hand-written notes of Allan Pinkerton's submissions and succeeded, partially, in losing myself in the stimulation of the intellectual endeavour. But after an only an hour, groaning gently in the hope of attracting some wifely attention,

I made my way up the stairs, one at a time, to bed. My neck was stiff and sore, one too many hurls in the Foursome with a particularly brawny advocate must have taken its toll and, for the first time since I had wed Laura, I felt my grand old age.

As the due date drew closer, I felt increasingly exhausted, worn out, I supposed, by my own fears. Drained of all energy. Yet, I was also in some paradoxical way zinging, crackling with joyful anticipation. The nursery was ready; painted pink on my insistence, though Laura let me know she thought I was jumping the gun. Imperial purple, she thought, covered all eventualities, but I vetoed that. The room had a delicate ivory-coloured cot by the window and a narrow frieze of Beatrix Potter animals adorned the four walls, running under the cornice. A little chest of drawers contained anything that up to ten babies might need, and I had compromised in that respect; blue, pink and white garments lay within, awaiting whoever might come to call. The doctor, a fashionable man recommended by Palmer (already father of nine) was booked for the home birth, and the monthly nurse was only a telephone call away.

My fearful state had left me on edge for the past few weeks. I both longed for the baby's arrival and was afraid of it. Suppose something went wrong for mother or child, or both? In every case that had come before me of obstetric negligence, the patient had succeeded in their claim; doctors were not infallible, nurses, too, made ghastly mistakes. Suddenly, post-partum haemorrhages seemed alarmingly commonplace, breech births resulting in shoulder dystocia (or death!) only too frequent and placenta previas an everyday event. Parturition, I realised, was hideously perilous, and its consequences, once matters as arcane to me as Ouija boards or corsetry, now obsessed me. In my gloomier, more sentimental moments, I had imagined my own journey towards death ('Beloved of nobody' on my marble headstone); now, it seemed miraculous that anyone completed that first momentous voyage alive. I wished my child could hatch from an egg.

Walking across the High Street, sweatily preoccupied and with my head down, I was nearly taken out by a pale blue Messerschmitt. Watching it zigzag its way down the cobbled High Street, my only thought was how unsuitable it would be for a family man.

As it was a Tuesday, Parliament House was buzzing with activity, bewigged advocates striding up and down the hall, solicitors and their anxious clients huddled together in the stalls considering offers to settle their cases, or the lack of them. I had been scheduled to sit in Court 5, on a case involving the sale of a large herd of 'gimmers' (virgin lady sheep to the uninitiated) who before their first taste of matrimonial bliss had, without exception, succumbed to some unexpected worm. Many thousands of pounds were at stake, but my clerk had mimed a yawn to warn me of what we had in store. An elderly man, clad head to foot in a rough tweed, was seated too near the open fire in the hall, and was sweating like a horse. Big hands, too. One of my litigious farmers, surely?

I watched from a discreet distance as his advocate, a well-known practitioner in agricultural law, paced the hall, side by side with his opponent, someone or other Hannan. My heart sank, as Hannan was known to have a kamikaze attitude to litigation, opting to crash and burn rather than capitulate, whatever the odds against him might be. Just as I was cursing under my breath, thinking the proof was bound to go ahead and tie me up for days, my clerk came rushing towards me, black gown flaring behind him, to tell me that our case had settled, and I was needed to attend to the formalities. The parties and their legal representatives were already in Court 5. Both farmers, I noted, wore city suits rather than the tweeds I had anticipated, and after a five-minute wrangle I was out again, and free as a bird, for the rest of the day.

After lunch, afraid to be too far from the city, we drove to Longniddry beach and sat in the Rover together hand in hand, looking out over the great, grey sea and listening to the waves break on the shore. Soon, we two would be three, and I think we were both acutely conscious of that fact.

'You will,' I said, ashamed to ask such a question 'still have some time for me?'

I was unused to exposing my soul, my innermost thoughts, but new fears assailed me daily.

'You are my life,' she replied immediately, squeezing my hand a little then raising it in her own and kissing my hairy knuckles.

I don't remember any more of our chat, just that we were, I felt, at that moment as close to each other as any two human beings upon this earth could be. Once I had existed, now I lived, and the world, and everything, everyone, in it had changed. Happiness is contagious,

I discovered, makes generosity easy, kindness easy, thoughtfulness easy, and not only to one's beloved. I do not want to overstate the case, but through her I had found a different way of being. One where people in shops chatted a little and I answered back; sometimes I caught the smile of a passer-by and returned it; one where I was normal, just normal. Not a crabbit outsider, dependent on the armour of a shamingly cruel wit, wherever I went. Laura loved people and they felt it, and reflected it back. And I had learnt my lessons from a master. Thanks to her, I had, belatedly, joined the human race.

We went to bed early that night; Laura found standing and sitting uncomfortable and was tired, her huge belly weighing her down. Her size was now such that simply looking at her made me long to sit down, and I say that as a man familiar with the technology of trouser expanders from their inception. Anyway, I wanted, as always, to be wherever she was, and as soon she put out her bedside lamp, I switched off my own. Worried that I might sleep through the first pangs of labour, or be too muzzy to react sensibly, I did not take my usual sleeping pill. To my regret, she lay facing away from me, her protuberance having prevented her for months from having her head close to mine; an intimacy I had loved since our earliest days.

# 4

I woke, unexpectedly, in the middle of the night and cursed myself for omitting the Mogadon. My neck was oddly painful and when I went to massage the muscles, I found it was also wet, sticky, to my touch. Hoping not to wake my beloved, I switched on my own light on to examine my dripping fingers and was alarmed to see my right-hand dark with my own blood. I felt the side of my neck again and sure enough it was bleeding. Laura turned to face me, her hand shielding her eyes from the bright light, and I glanced at her sleepy face. Her mouth was glistening with blood and, unthinkingly, my fingers returned to my neck, alighting on two little puncture holes. Hoping I was still asleep, locked in a particularly vivid nightmare, I rose shakily and went to the bathroom. I turned my neck to one side and saw the two little marks, and moving closer to the mirror to get a better look only confirmed that first impression. A haunted face, one the colour of chalk, stared back at me. On my return to the bedroom, Laura was sitting up, one hand cradled protectively around her pregnant belly.

'Are you alright, my love?' she asked, eyes still heavy from sleep.

'No, decidedly not,' I replied, moving no closer to the bed.

'What's the matter?' she said, an anxious expression on her face, having picked up, I have no doubt, my own uncharacteristically sharp tone.

'You,' I said, unable to believe what I was saying, 'have bitten me, pierced me, punctured my neck, drained it of blood like a vampire. Laura, my blood is all over your mouth, your cheek. It is dribbling down your chin.'

At the word 'vampire' her head dropped, and she cried out as if I had struck her. But, and I noted this even then, she did not question my assertion, did not deny it. That is how the innocent and truthful would have responded. Old habits, as I said earlier, die hard. In reality, how could she deny those twin punctures? My life blood was all over her. With the shock of what had happened, I found myself trembling, my teeth chattering audibly. Cold. I climbed back into bed, making sure that my flesh did not touch her flesh.

'Well? What have you to say?' I demanded, awaiting an answer. Then I remembered how tired I had often felt of late, how lethargic, and it dawned on me, with horror, why that might be.

'You,' and I could hardly get the words out, 'you . . . have done this before, previously, haven't you? You have drunk . . . drained . . . my blood before?'

Still she said not a word, but her bowed head gave an almost imperceptible nod. I suddenly felt dizzy, tired and unimaginably sad. Waves of melancholy arose from nowhere and engulfed me, overwhelmed me. My love, my new life, had all been an illusion, a delusion; something literally too good to be true. In the suffocating, inky blackness that now engulfed me, I felt trapped, bereft of all hope, as if I would never rise up to the light again, never reach the surface. Tears began to pour down my cheeks and, involuntarily, I let out a loud sob. How had this come to pass, how had this unbelievable thing happened? Immediately, she put her arms around me, and feeling the embrace, her soft skin, I knew that whatever she had done, for the moment I did not care; I wept against her breast, unable to stop myself and careless of everything except her presence. Childlike.

'My darling,' she said, resting her chin on my balding pate. We remained so entwined for many minutes, in silence, then I broke it, asking, 'Laura, my beloved, why did you do that? Why would you?'

'I am so sorry, Jock. Words cannot express how sorry. I couldn't resist, the impulse was too powerful for me; I was too weak.'

'Impulse? What impulse? What are you talking about?'

'You called me some kind of vampire. I am some kind of vampire; I hate it but it's what I am.'

'Don't be ridiculous,' I said, getting up abruptly and sitting on the side of the bed, 'You're not a vampire! Vampires don't exist. I was just calling you that . . . that word, using the word as a sort of shorthand; I didn't mean it. Of course you're not a vampire, they're the stuff of legends, penny-dreadfuls. Heavens, you'll tell me next that you can fly!'

'Of course, I can't fly. But I do know what I am. I am a vampire.' Now she was sitting close beside me.

'Darling, speak sense to me, please,' I begged, taking both her hands in mine and continuing, gibbering like a lunatic man in my shock, 'I know you drank my blood. How very odd that sounds! I never thought I would be saying something so . . . so surreal . . . so gothic . . . but it is probably that strange pregnancy phenomenon. What is it called? Pica, that's it. I had a case when I was devilling, a woman eating raw potatoes. Is it called geomelophagia, is that the term? She was so obsessional that she stole them from the nearby greengrocer's shop. Some pregnant women eat coal, eels or is it lampreys, don't they? Whole gingerbreads? It is simply a vitamin deficiency. Low haemoglobin or anaemia. I don't know what exact deficiency craving blood indicates, but what I do know is that vampires, werewolves, Frankenstein's monster . . . none of them exist. Bram Stoker made all it up. You're not a "vampire". Forgive me calling you that silly, silly word, I didn't mean it, darling. But let's not make this worse than it already is. We'll work this out between us . . .'

'I drank your blood before . . . before I was . . . we were expecting a baby,' she said, interrupting me.

'Before . . .' The wind was quite taken from my sails.

'Yes. Before.'

'So, were you . . . what . . . are you going to kill me? Have you killed people? Your last husband?' I was joking; it was ludicrous, preposterous, but if it was true?

'No!' she exclaimed, sounding shocked, so utterly appalled at the idea that I let out an involuntary little giggle, a slightly hysterical sound. I was lost, compass-less in some strange, dark land.

'I wouldn't kill you; I wouldn't harm you! I love you, you know that. You can't doubt that. I only take blood from those I love . . . and I ceased to love my last husband. You know he's alive, you heard our divorce. He was sitting at the back of the court.'

Alarmingly, she was taking all my questions seriously, answering them seriously as if we were talking sense; talking about the weather or the price of milk. And she neither sounded, nor looked, like a mad woman. I felt a slight chill, a sense of confusion, of unreality. The ground beneath me seemed no longer solid. It was developing fine, hairline cracks, fracturing below my feet, and I did not want to fall into an abyss with her, disappear into a folie à deux, hurtle together into a black hole.

'Have you killed people?'

'Jock, remember you can kill, too. Have you killed? What sort of a thing is that to ask me?'

I looked at her beautiful face, into those blue, blue eyes.

'Our child!' I said, a grotesque thought having suddenly hit me, 'You'll love her. Will she be in danger from you?'

Saying it out loud, the question sounded even more bizarre. I opened my eyes wide to show how outlandish a suggestion I thought it was, one so far-fetched that a laugh could surely be the only response. But I waited in anguish for her reply.

'Of course not. Only those I love romantically, truly love. Only them, I promise you, Jock.'

'Why? Can't you control yourself?' I asked, finding myself drawn in by her strange logic and, I suppose, being pulled into the fantasy more deeply or, possibly, humouring her. What else could I do? Words might provide a guiding light, a way out of this starless space.

'It's a compulsion – the more I love, the more tempted, no, compelled, I am. My father told me that we can take an earthly life . . . but, as I said, so can you. What I mean is that we could drain all of someone's blood, literally, but I never have. If I did do that, then, he said, my victim . . . my victim would not die, not be killed. In fact, they, like me, would live forever. However long that is supposed to be.'

'And our child?'

'What about our child?'

'What will our child be?'

'Our child will be like me and like you. It will be our child.'

'Not an eternal freak, a bloodsucker?'

Exasperated, I was beginning to lose patience and, thought, foolishly, that she might be shocked back into reality, into our old, recognisable, domestic and comfortable world. Into normality, in short.

'You have never been unkind before,' she said, edging almost imperceptibly away from me.

'Unkind? I was not aware before that you were a vampire or, frankly, delusional, insane, or whatever you are, because you didn't think to tell me. If you are a "vampire", don't you think I should have been warned by you before I married you, before we conceived a child?'

In my bewilderment, I seemed to have joined her, wading out of my depth with her, the icy waters closing above me.

She bowed her head, covering her face with her hands, sighing audibly.

'When?' she asked, looking steadily at me.

'When what?' I replied.

'When should I have told you? Before we fell in love?'

'Certainly!'

'For a professional judge you take in surprisingly little. I didn't come in search of you. You, you have often told me with pride, came in search of me. Found me. You know when you fell in love, but you have no idea when I fell in love because you have never asked.'

'Well, well, maybe . . .' I blustered.

'I loved you from the start, and I have a heart just the same as you. Vampirism, it's like, like a disease or something. But worse, of course, in so many ways. But think for a second. When you first meet someone, do you tell them you have, say, Hepatitis C? Do you have to? Are you duty-bound? If I told casual friends, acquaintances, I was a vampire, I'd have been locked up in asylum long ago, and, as I explained, I feel no compulsion with them. I don't want to drink their blood. Only once I am in love, and by then . . . by then . . . I AM in love. I think I'll resist. I convince myself I'll resist. And if I resist, what have I to tell? If I resist, I am not a . . . a vampire.'

'Call me pedantic but, yes, you are. The rest of us are not eternal as you, apparently, are. Why, in heaven's name, did you not tell me!'

'I have just told you why, tried to explain. Can't you see the paradox? Unless I'm in love there is nothing to tell. Acquaintances don't care if one's run over by a bus tomorrow. I'm under no duty to tell them how long I may live. Am I? Once I'm in love, I believe that there's nothing to tell. I convince myself, I suppose, but the truth is the more I love, the more the compulsion grows. I only take a little. Like most lovers, I didn't tell you my secret because I would have lost you. I would have lost you, wouldn't I?'

'No.'

'You would have married a vampire?'

'Oh, for Heaven's sake, Laura! You don't shrivel up or burn when exposed to the sun, we got married practically standing under a crucifix. You eat garlic. Bats don't congregate around you, fly in and out of our windows! Why not? I don't understand! This is all balderdash, madness, total and complete tripe!' In my exasperation, my confusion, I couldn't help it, I shouted at her. 'Stop it!'

God knows, in my youth I watched Nosferatu alone more than once, and a few bat-ridden imitations featuring a fanged Christopher Lee. What about all those picturesque tropes? Had Hammer Horror some sort of insight unavailable to the rest of mankind? Or had they got it wrong? But it was a story, a tale, fiction. There was no wrong. Oh, why was she having such sport, such cruel sport with me? I was tired, it was the middle of the night, my neck hurt. Surely, she would, too damn late, laugh it off now. Make it go away.

'Nor do I understand it. I have no idea. But things change, living things change. Most people have a palmaris longus muscle, but some don't. Evolution occurs amongst all living creatures. With us, too, I suppose. My father told me all I know. He said that we can make people live like us, live forever, though I never have. He said our family was different.'

'Different! I'll say!'

Another sudden dreadful thought struck me, made me wince with pain.

'Have you loved before, drunk your love's blood before?'

She did not answer.

'Well? Have you? Am I the first, am I the only one?' I demanded.

'I have lived a long, unimaginably long life. I have loved before but, and here, Jock, you won't believe me: I have never loved anyone as much as I love you.'

'Me!' I couldn't believe my ears. That did it. Whatever else was true, that had to be a lie. My unlovability had been a constant in my life, an ever-fixed mark. A weakness of mine was being exploited; a new reality was being foisted upon me.

Seeing a drip running down my neck, she wiped the blood from her own face with an end of her silk nightie and moved closer as if to tend me. Instinctively, I ducked, and this time I saw a look of pain cross her face.

'I wouldn't hurt you!'

'Your father? That will be the long-dead father that you told me about? Oh, and possibly the dead mother that couldn't make it to our wedding? Maybe, dead or undead, they both did . . . what . . . flap up the aisle, hang upside-down on a nearby rafter?'

'Jock, I am sorry. They do not age. They look young, like me.'

I wrinkled my nose in disgust at the very idea of such a family.

'So, you lied to me to solve the problem!'

She grimaced a little, a muscle in her jaw working, as if to distract from pain. But observing it I took no heed, too absorbed in myself, in my own hurt, to care. Too angry. I saw myself for what I was. A fat old fool. She had never loved me, probably just needed me to procreate and pay for the pair of them. All lies, it had all been lies. I had fallen for a beautiful parasite.

'You,' I said, shaking again with emotion, 'whatever you say now, never loved me. You used me for my money!'

I did not mean to, but I released a low, primeval howl of anguish.

'This, all this, only happened precisely because I loved you. Love you.' She put her arms around me, but, afraid, this time I shrank from her touch.

'I am,' she continued, evidently shocked by my withdrawal, stuttering a little, 'as you may recollect from the divorce, not a pauper. Quite the opposite. I still have my house in the Grange. I have had other suitors, men obsessed with me . . . I could easily have found someone with whom to father a child, to marry even. Jock, I love you, loved you, despite our ages, despite your appearance and your dreadful self-doubts about it. I had never met someone like you, you are all the things I have told you. Can nothing shake your belief in your own complete unlovability? My sweet, you are so childlike in your need for love, so parched, so lovable.'

'No,' I said frostily, 'I am an old fool, and it is an old story.'

For the first time since I had sat down on the bed, I looked at her properly. Tears glistened on those wonderful cheekbones, overflowed from her pale eyes, and her face was distorted with a sort of grief, a sort of desperation. I hardened my heart and rose stiffly from our bed, although I was not sure what I was going to do next. Instinctively, I suppose, I needed to put some distance, literally, between us. Looking down at the sheet on the bed, I realised it was now a pale pink colour, and the stain was spreading like a sunrise as I watched.

'Christ! Your waters?' I said, panic rising.

'My waters,' she replied in a tone as sombre as if announcing a death. I rushed to the phone and within ten minutes, no more, Dr Robarts had arrived and installed himself in our room with his bag of tricks. Closing the bedroom door, I went down to my study and poured myself a large glass of Glenfiddich.

# 5

In the study, tucked away behind the drawing room, I would not hear a sound. Drummond Place could be reduced to rubble, London Road bombed and Scotland Street aflame, but silence would continue to reign in that cosy, book-lined den. I sat in my favourite armchair, immobile, for ten long minutes. Then, unable to bear the thought of my love in agony, bringing forth our child, I rose, unable to insulate myself, isolate myself from her a minute longer. I looked around for somewhere suitable to station myself and settled on the bottom of the stair, whisky tumbler in hand.

Nothing escaped me from that listening post and I felt, in a strange and probably laughable way, that hearing those awful animal noises I was suffering with her. Truly, if I could have taken that cup from her, drunk of it in her stead, I would have done so. Sometimes, cringing, having instinctively put my hands to my ears, unable to listen to anymore, I almost crawled back to the tomb-like silence of the study. Twice after hearing a high, roaring scream I rushed up the stairs, tore along the passage to our bedroom door and raised my knuckle, ready to demand entry. But, within, I heard a low, calm voice and a breathless answer, neither of which suggested either a birth or a death. At about midnight the doctor came downstairs, sweat on his brow and his waistcoat buttons undone, but only to reassure me that, despite everything, all was going exactly to plan, and that there was nothing to worry about. It was a normal labour. Eyes aching with tiredness, I nodded, then raised my empty glass to him as if in some parody of a toast. In his glance I thought I saw distaste.

My thoughts gave me no peace while that infant was struggling to be born. Something which, a lifetime ago, had seemed so natural, so uncomplicated, so everyday and ordinary, now made me clutch my head, unable to fathom any longer what to think or what to do. Laura, whatever name I had called her, or she had chosen for herself, had, as a matter of fact, lapped blood from my neck. Not once, as might (and I stress 'might') be explained by some aberrant craving resulting from her pregnant state, but more than once, including before she became pregnant. Vampire was the actual word she had used to describe herself. What other one fitted? My baby, my longed-for child, might be whatever her mother was. If Laura was mad, and other than in her bloodsucking habit I had seen no sign of it, my little darling might inherit that, or some even more florid form of insanity. In this fresh Hell, that would be the lesser evil. All I had wanted was a baby, a harmless, wide-eyed, gurgling little human. Not a monster or a mad woman. Alone in my Gethsemane, in the silence of my head, I howled like a banshee.

For an instant, my mother's face loomed into view, an expression of repugnance contorting her perfect features as she looked into my eyes. Her coldness, her eventual disenchantment with me could be explained. She had witnessed a baby, her only child, transform itself into a hideous juvenile shoebill. Something no one, not even a mother, could love. I laughed out loud. Now something much worse was forcing its hunched way through living flesh as it attempted to storm her bloodline. Some kind of freak, possibly a malformed cross-breed unintended by nature, would soon be swaddled in the tiny Belgian lace nightie ('Duchess' lace, no less) so treasured by her. Maybe it would be better that the thing, the child, was not born alive? And its mother, too, was beauty incarnate. History was repeating itself.

A merciful stillbirth might be devoutly to be wished. At such a dreadful thought, my heart cried out that the child was mine, my child, to love and to be loved by. I should be her protector. This mite was the carrier of all my hopes, my dreams, was the fruit of our love. I would shield her from the world. As I was agonising, my mind spinning with contradictory thoughts, I heard a high-pitched scream. It was followed by total silence. A heavy silence, as if the world and every creature in it was holding its breath. I waited one minute and then stomped up the stair.

Inside the bedroom, I made out my wife cradling our baby to her breast. Light from the lamp fell on the pair of them, illuminating them against the background gloom and conjuring up, for all the world, a centuries-old sacred image; that of the Madonna and child. I rushed up to Laura, desperate to see our infant, all worries, fears and anxieties forgotten, made joyful by the miracle of birth. I would protect her against any harm, every harm, until my heart ceased to beat. The sweet domesticity of the scene brought tears to my eyes. Somewhere in the surrounding dark, the doctor, jacket back on, was wrapping some instrument or other in a small white sheet.

Secretly, I longed to hold my child.

The babe's eyes were shut, and it made no noise. Close to, I could see it was perfectly formed in every respect, from its rounded little features to its miniscule fingers and toes. I was taken aback by its tininess, and its fine fair hair. But it was also limp, floppy as a ragdoll, and had an unnatural grey complexion. My baby made no movement, and shifting my gaze to Laura's drawn face, alarmed, I saw that, hugging the child to her, tears were running down her cheeks too and splashing onto its perfectly rounded head.

'Laura?'

'Dead,' was all she replied, pressing the tiny body closer to her and lowering her face to touch the child's cold cheek with her own, as if to pass her own vital warmth on through her skin.

'I'm very sorry, my Lord,' Dr Robarts said, closing his Gladstone bag beside me with a click, loud as a gunshot.

'What?'

I had not been aware that he had joined us.

'I did everything I could to try and bring her back to life. But it was not meant to be. I don't know why this happened, but nature simply did not intend this little girl to live.'

'No,' I said bitterly, 'I understand. I am sure you did do everything in your power for my wife, Doctor, and our child. Thank you for all you have done.'

'Some souls are not destined to make the journey, not strong enough . . .'

I did not reply.

'Look after your wife, it's been an interminably long and arduous night and she's suffered much pain and distress for nothing. Lost a fair bit of blood, too. And there's no new life to take her mind off it, make it all go away.'

At his words, I felt an overpowering urge to embrace Laura, take her in my arms and wipe away her tears, but I resisted. Instead, as the doctor had suggested, I went downstairs and phoned the undertakers and, in less than an hour, they had arrived. Before they came I cut off a lock of my daughter's hair, found a small envelope and slipped it into my wallet. Our child had proved to be all too mortal.

At 9 am, having brushed my shoes, I left the house as usual. The nurse had arrived at 7.30 and was with Laura, attending to her needs. As I walked along Princes Street, I rehearsed the response I would give anyone who asked me about the birth or congratulated me on the new baby.

'Sadly, she was stillborn,' I repeated inwardly, accustoming myself to the word, and in my mind sliding away from my imaginary interlocutor in order to prevent any further chatter on the subject. My plan was to go immediately to my own chamber, close the door and fend off any attempts to enter by conjuring up an important incoming phone call. With luck that would ensure that I saw nobody. What I would do, alone in my office, I did not know. But, to be frank, I could not be at home with her. However, as every Scot knows, 'The best laid schemes o' mice and men gang aft a-gley'.

No sooner was I through the door of Parliament House than my clerk clattered breathlessly up to me, anxious to hear the news. Kenny had a bottle of Scotch riding on my firstborn being a boy. Already a father of four, he was an old hand and swore by some witch's, or midwife's, lore about the shape of the bulge. Many a time he had reassured me that Laura would come through it just fine, 'tickety-boo', and that 'for all their noise', childbirth was what women were designed for and that despite the racket and gore it would be, to quote again, 'A piece of cake'.

'Maybe Walnut Cream Hand or Victoria Sponge Hand, or for a boy, Black Forest Hand?' Laura had quipped on hearing his prediction. That had been only a week earlier, but it felt an age away.

'I didn't expect to see you in, my Lord. Boy? Girl?' he asked, eyes wide.

I felt my face freeze as I intoned 'Stillborn girl', forcing my lips to mouth such sombre words. I watched him rearrange his face and, because I was so familiar with him, I knew he would be wondering what on earth I was doing here instead of being at home with my poor wife. Comforting, tending to her. You see, none of the staff could have been in any doubt about my infatuation; I could not hide it. My face lit up when I mentioned Laura, I felt myself smiling inwardly at the sound of her name. My voice too, I was aware, in some intangible way caressed her name as I spoke it. And, somehow, whatever we were discussing, I invariably brought the conversation round to her. I was, I daresay, a bit of a laughing-stock, although I had thought that a small price up until that day.

'I'm very sorry to hear that, my Lord.'

'Indeed.'

As I marched at twice my normal speed through that rabbit warren of a building, I prayed that he would pass the news on and that I should not have to intone that dreadful word to another soul. I need not have worried. In that place, gossip travelled as freely as smoke in the air. Twice, I dodged a colleague; the WC provided a refuge from one and a sidestep worthy of a fly half saved me from facing another. All the time, my legs were trembling. I felt, if I am honest, as fragile as glass, as if I might shatter into a thousand pieces.

In the sanctuary of my room, a tower of assorted legal volumes in front of me, I covered my face with my hands. My poor little girl. I, her own father, had been ambivalent about her arrival, had not wished wholeheartedly that she would make safe passage into this dark and dangerous world. And as the little scrap was forcing herself towards her life, reaching for me and gasping for air, had I been praying to the Almighty for her arrival, willing her to survive in that new, unfamiliar element? Not a bit of it. The prospect of her death had been entertained by me before she was even born. 'Entertained'? No, wished for, hoped for. Wicked, unbearably wicked. What kind of monster did that make me?

I wept, ashamed and bereft in equal measure. At least I had something left of her, I comforted myself, fingering my wallet in my inside pocket and visualising her soft hair within. Unable to resist, I took out the envelope, and as I opened it a sunbeam caught the contents, turning the hair flaxen. My child had been as comely as her mother, and, thinking about them both I howled, for the loss of the babe, for Laura's agony and my own broken dreams. Our child would never know her own name. Had never uttered a sound, had no present nor future, and I would not cheer her on as she ran the egg-and-spoon race, pigtails flying, or carry her over my shoulder, sleepy to bed, or watch her put on her wedding veil. There was no miraculous being for me to love and protect, cherish come what may. The world could not be put to rights, made anew, its old cruelties washed away. And in the pitifully few minutes of life granted to my child, her whole life, I had let her down.

'My Lord, are you alright?' Kenny, unbeknownst to me, must have caught my howl and come to see that no harm had befallen me.

'Fine, fine. Thank you, Kenny,' I replied, opening the volume of Session Cases in front of me and looking at the right-hand page, though I could see nothing of the text.

'I know what's it like, Marion lost a baby too. A good while ago now.'

'I'm very sorry to hear that, Kenny. I hope that, if you told me at the time, I was sympathetic to you?' I did not raise my head. To my mortification, I had no recollection of this confidence.

'Very, my Lord. I appreciated it a great deal. You had flowers sent to Marion, white roses as I recall. Her favourite.'

'If,' I said, feeling old, and aware of my own lifeless tone, 'I had understood then what I understand now, I would have sent her much more than a few flowers. So, I am sorry for that insensitivity. Now, I really must finish writing my judgement in the Health Board case.' I looked up at the man, and though he could not fail to take in my wet cheeks, I prayed he would also realise that I was desperate to be on my own again. Thankfully, he did, and murmuring something about checking something with the General Department, he disappeared as quickly as he had come. Alone again, I forced my head to batter my heart into shape.

By lunchtime I had got sufficient grip on myself to go and register the death. Once all the forms had been filled in, teeth gritted, I set off on foot for Bruntsfield and the undertakers' establishment. At Purves, I was taken under the wing of a kindly hen of a woman who seemed to know who I was without my saying a word. Disconcertingly, the black eyes of my bustling little helper were level with my lowest waistcoat button. From her accent, I'd hazard she hailed originally from Buckie.

'Just the wee coffin with brass handles, sir?' she asked softly, gazing up at me.

'Yes.'

'And what would you like the bairn to wear?'

That threw me. A cloth of gold.

My mind drifted back to the bright, sunny day on which Laura and I had gone in search of the baby's trousseau, or is it called a layette? One or other. I know there is some arcane technical term used by the baby-literate. We had ended up in Jenners, fingering what, before I saw our minute child, appeared to me to be dolly's clothes.

'For the boy,' Laura had said with total assurance, holding some light-blue knitted bonnet-like thing up for my inspection.

'Correction: girl,' I replied, taking it gently from her and substituting something similar but in pink.

'Maybe,' the bored shop assistant said, spectacles and chain dangling off her ample bosom, 'it'll be twins. One of each.' A queue was forming behind us, but a smartly dressed man, possibly a floor walker, waved to the other customers, signalling for them to go to another till.

'Mauve, no, purple, would be a compromise?' Laura suggested.

'We'll have the blue,' I said, handing the thing to the assistant, baffled, as I often was, by Laura's logic and wondering what such a compromise represented.

'And the pink,' she said, handing that item to the woman as well.

Back in the funeral parlour, the assistant was still looking at me, expecting an answer.

'The bairn should wear . . .' I mumbled, my voice on the edge of breaking, 'something pink. Anything pink. Whatever you have.'

I spent the rest of the afternoon in the New Club. A couple of the members asked me about the baby, but most had either never known about the forthcoming birth or, if they had, had forgotten. A shortage in the supply of Ballater black pudding would likely have caused more consternation, and my knowledge of that fact was a relief. Sympathy would have unmanned me. Hidden behind my *Times* I was safe; the sponge-bag trousers and shiny black brogues poking out could have belonged to anyone. In an attempt to distract myself I scanned a few columns of the newspaper but, for all I took in, they could have been written in braille. At four o' clock on the dot, I left the club and meandered slowly up Hanover Street, then down, past Queen Street Gardens. Usually, catching sight of the lit windows of my home made me speed up, drawn like a moth towards the light. But that night I stood outside my own front door, the rain ricocheting off the crown of my bowler, and after five minutes, I had to force myself to cross my own threshold.

Laura was upstairs, in our bed. I sat on the edge of it, yearning to take her hand in mine. It was resting on the scarlet silk eiderdown and close enough for me to touch. But something held me back and I let it lie there. I could hear the monthly nurse, her main purpose now redundant, rattling about with crockery, laying the table for my tea in the dining room below.

'Jock,' Laura said, 'my darling, I am so sorry.'

Hearing that pitiful, undeserved apology, my heart almost burst and, instinctively, I stretched for her hand, but immediately an urgent voice in my head, which had been busy whispering to me on and off all day, reminded me what she had done. She had drunk my blood. I put my hand back on my own knee. As a child I had read to myself, many times, a Scottish legend called 'Morag and the Water Horse' and it had, invariably, scared me witless. The water horse, a terrible creature that dwelt in the loch, could assume any form: aged woman, black raven or whatever it desired, and in that form, it would get close enough to its quarry (usually a beautiful young maid) and 'mercilessly devour its prey'.

My mother, finding me shivering, reading the story in bed had said, perhaps imagining it would reassure me: 'A lovely young maid? You'll be quite safe, Jock.

Even a water horse draws the line somewhere!' Her words were of no comfort.

Morag, doing her spinning by the loch side, waiting to call in the browsing cattle, is approached by a young, attractive youth and, somehow, she ends up with his head in her lap whilst she combs his dripping locks. Only when her comb becomes 'choked with fine green strands of weed and grains of silt' does 'terror enter her soul'. Actually, she escapes the creature's maw by crossing a burn – running water, in most legends, being uncrossable by fiends. No one could mistake me for Morag, but every time I looked at Laura, I thought of that shape-shifting water horse. No burn ran through our house and the puncture wounds in my neck told their own story. Feeling I was becoming slightly unhinged, had lost not just my bearings but the fixed points of my compass, I steeled myself and, finally, picked up her limp white hand and raised it to my lips.

'You must rest, my love, get your strength back. I'll sleep in the spare room tonight, let you recover. Now, is there anything I can get you? Flowers, cordials, grapes? Anything?'

This time yesterday, I thought ruefully, I would have needed no cause or excuse to strew our bed with hundreds of the most expensive roses I could find. I would have been wanton with their crimson petals. Today, to her sickbed, I brought only offers and, if I am honest, my heart was not even in them. Below the tangle of stiff collars in one of my dressing-room drawers lay a necklace of rubies and pearls; something fished, months earlier, from the backroom safe by my little bombazine-clad acquaintance in the jeweller's shop.

Many times I had imagined myself placing it around Laura's swan neck as the nurse, silhouetted in the window, rocked our daughter in her plump arms. It was destined for the mother of our firstborn.

Shaking her head, she turned her face to the pillow and we both knew I had been dismissed.

From then onwards, I never again slept a night with my wife. I do not say we did not make love, we did, and it brought us closer together and I was grateful, much relieved, that the sexual side of our marriage had not ended. But, in that lovely somnolent haze before one closes one's eyes in sleep, I never felt her head beside mine, never moulded my inelegant, misshapen body around her warm form. And I missed it and all the other unthinking intimacies born of a shared bed.

I loved her no less. But that love was no longer simple, natural.

# 6

Late in spring that same year, we were on holiday in Cyprus, staying in a villa near Saint Hilarion Castle in the Kyrenia mountains. I thought the beauty of the place might heal her, help her come to terms with the loss of our baby, and, strange as it might seem for an atheist, I have a schoolboy interest in the painted churches of Cyprus. Byzantine architecture, too. A close friend of my mother (and, like her, formerly a society Blackshirt and acolyte of St Unity) had, before I became puer non gratus in my own house, amused me with tales of donkeys, digs and, thrillingly for a small boy, the wonder of coprolites.

Consequently, I had been holidaying on the island on my own for many years and knew it well. I had also arranged to meet up with an elderly, strikingly hirsute friend of mine, Dr Vassos Spyridakis, so that he could show us the monastery of Saint John Lampadistis in Kalopanagiotis in the Troodos mountains. A murder of crows, I had warned Laura, could hide in his great black beard.

'Is there a Mrs Spyridakis?' she asked as we sat down to dinner.

'Only another aged Dr Spyridakis.'

'A brother? With as good a beard?'

'A wife, but Maria's is only a one-crow beard. You

know, the sort of thing I myself might manage,' I replied, stroking my own soft cheeks with my hands.

On our first morning and, foolishly, given the baking midday heat, we had walked a couple of miles on melting tarmac in the direction of Bellapaise. The sound of the bells drew us towards the village and, hot and thirsty, we drank Soumada in the shade of a grove of cypresses below the ruined Abbey. But less than a mile out on our return journey, I found myself exhausted, breathless and sweaty. Laura was worried about me. So we stopped in an orchard close to the road, the ground white as snow with fallen orange blossoms, their heady scent filling the air. We sat leaning against each other on the perfumed carpet, and I must have, although I have no memory of it, lain down and gone to sleep. I woke, with Laura, eyes shut, curled up beside me. My neck stung, and my questing fingers came back wet. As before, I noticed blood on her face although, this time, only a trace at the side of her mouth. Whilst my mind turned to thoughts of the water horse, I felt, odd – outrageous even – as it may sound, the faintest hint of reassurance.

Love explained it.

Not only did I love her; she also loved me. Here was the proof. You see, I had listened to what she had told me on that awful night, in fact, found myself reliving it all too often. 'The more I love, the more the compulsion grows.'

The urge was irresistible. I was irresistible. And that is a sentence I never expected to write.

It took an immense effort, but I said nothing about it to her once she woke. What was the point? One might as well rebuke a crocodile for being a crocodile or praise a fawn for being a fawn. Also, and this has a bearing, I did not feel too much weakened by her picnic. Whatever blood she had taken, she had done me no real physical harm. Later, contemplating the act, I felt a shiver of repugnance throughout my entire body, but no longer the horror I experienced on that first occasion. Given time, can one accustom oneself to anything?

But, as I have told you, things had changed. In fact, and I am loathe to admit this even to myself, I found that I resented my love for Laura more and more as each month passed. I was afraid of it. BL, law had been my life, all in all to me. AL, faced with four days in the Appeal Court adjudicating on a dispute as to the exact meaning of 'Crown Property' in a statute, I tried, if you can believe it, to dodge the allocation. Once I would have been amongst the most sharp-elbowed, the most ruthless in attempting to snatch such a choice titbit. Even a case on the indicia of the Contract of Partnership did not make my juices run. The joy of my retirement, a mere fifteen years or so hence, was to be the writing of a textbook, my magnum opus, its putative title being Hand on Partnership. My enthusiasm for these matters had crumbled to ash, yet, before her, it and only it had given savour to my life.

I no longer recognised myself.

And I understood why. I had become an addict. Like some emaciated junkie, shovelling cocaine up his nostrils in a lavatory, I loved the drug, the white powder, but was frightened of the addiction and its effects. But it was worse than that, much, much worse. Never mind me and my willpower; what if my beautiful drug gave me up?

I could not bear the thought. I decided I must reduce my dependence on my wife.

Once upon a time, we had done everything together. Now, coldly, calculatedly, I took to doing things on my own; galleries, gardens, lectures, castles, concerts and so on. I might as well have been footloose and fancy-free; an unloved and lonely bachelor again. But the truth is that listening to Glen Campbell's 'Gentle on my Mind' and 'Galveston' at the Usher Hall or gawping at Demarco's latest naked or paint-splattered 'Happening' in the festival, I longed for Laura by my side. Without her beside me, whatever I saw or heard, I could no longer take any relish in it. Rothko's colours had not changed; Eardley's tumultuous seas continued to assault the cliffs. But I felt nothing. Daunted, I persevered, thinking I must simply accustom myself to this new state of affairs, and the relative contentment of my single days would return. Once, in accordance with my own self-imposed diktat, I was patrolling the Hanover Gallery, pretending to squint at some Indian miniatures in the hushed dark, when I bumped into Evan Palmer, looking I thought, uncharacteristically scruffy.

'And where,' he said, eyes scanning the room too eagerly, 'is the lovely Lady Hand?' Monomania, I suspect, may well be the secret behind the success of apex predators such as the shark.

'Laura is at a talk in the Botanical Gardens,' I replied primly.

'On her own?'

'Yes.'

'Someone like her? Not for long, Jock, not for long!' he replied, tapping the side of his nose to indicate, I think, his worldly wisdom. Without showing it, I felt a frisson of fear run the length of my spine. Did he imagine I was not aware of my own vulnerability; a shoebill in love with a swan? In a world of swans. I was tortured by it. Think what fun Hans Christian Andersen would have had with it! A broken-hearted shoebill would be found dead in a ditch, having accidently caught his own reflection in splash of horse piss. But hearing my innermost anxieties confirmed by such a man, I felt a tidal wave of hopelessness engulf me, overpower me. To survive, somehow I had to prepare myself for life after Laura; no, life without Laura.

'Watch out for those horny-handed sons of the soil. Horny-handed, I say, so take heed!'

'And the present Lady Palmer? Is she here somewhere?' Hell, for all I cared, but I needed to change the subject.

'The former Lady Palmer, actually. No. All the riches of the St Margaret's Retail Park inquiry could not keep that money-loving little creature by my side. Anyway, she hates art.'

'I'm sorry, Evan.'

'Don't be, old boy. Really. Unlike you, I'm as shallow as a puddle.'

I forced myself to finish my inspection of the exhibits before driving to Inverleith Road to wait in the car for her. Antennae twitching, I scanned the gates for

Palmer, but either he had gone in search of other prey or, possibly, I was slowly but surely going insane.

I carried on with my strategy, ignoring my ever-present doubts but unable to dispel them. I bought my love a dog (a King Charles spaniel named Oliver), but despite her pleas, declined to walk it with her in Inverleith Park or, God forbid, up Arthur's Seat. I was, I explained, too busy, and, as I did not need to explain, too fat. Without me or a child to occupy her, time passed slowly for Laura. Knowing that, I encouraged her to return to drawing classes, suggesting she take a girlfriend with her. To encourage her to enrol at the University for evening classes, I brought back a prospectus and a mass of pink forms. And, like the sweet person she was, she accepted our new regime and did her best to reshape her own life to accommodate my wishes.

'Come with me, Jock?' she often begged, but I always relied on the same tired excuse. My work. At times, it felt as if she was deep under water, and every time she managed to bob up to the surface for air, I forced her head down, back below the waves. I wonder if I was punishing her in some way; I did not think so at the time.

One evening when we were having dinner together and had just finished a miraculously aerated chocolate soufflé, I saw her look at me then sit up, as if straightening or stiffening her spine. My pudgy fingers were, as so often, fondling my fourth glass of riesling, and, perhaps, I was a bit slow off the mark. Drink calmed my overactive mind.

'Jock, we could have another one, you know?'

‘Soufflé? No, darling, far too rich for me. Besides, I don’t want to burst out of my robes like old McIntosh. Split at the back. I heard his Macer, seeing him sitting on the Bench, refer to him as Grumpy Humpty Dumpty. No, not another mouthful for me.’

‘Another baby, we could try for another baby. I’d love one. You so wanted one?’

‘No,’ I said, finally, realizing what she meant.

‘You,’ she persisted, looking at me with her beautiful blue eyes, ‘were happier than I have ever seen you last time. You told me you’d always dreamt of having a child. We could have a child.’

I think she was begging me, understood what I did not understand.

‘No,’ I repeated, folding my napkin and rising from the table, signalling that all discussion was over.

‘Why not?’

‘Because,’ I said slowly, ‘I wanted, I thought we wanted . . . a child. Not a freak.’

‘Like me,’ she replied quietly, adding, ‘But, of course, that child would not be a freak to me.’

‘Unlike me?’ I said, detecting an unexpected implication. She did not answer.

‘Well,’ I continued, ‘I am a freak to you, am I not? Is that not what you are reminding me?’

‘In your turn, yes. But I wouldn’t have put it that way. I love you, wanted to have your child. Want to have our child.’

‘Oh, did you, did you . . . do you . . . do you, indeed?’ I said, blustering, muttering the first thing that came into my head, as I walked to the door and hastily let myself out of the kitchen. What could I say? Unlikely as it might seem, I had not, even once, viewed matters from her perspective. Why should I? I had not been caught lapping up her blood. I was the normal one. I did, so to speak, what it said on the tin. No explanations were needed from me.

In my study, having poured myself a port, I settled into my armchair by the fireside. The nasty little voice in my head, admittedly, as woozy and incapable of clear thinking as I was, was working overtime, making things worse, chattering away to himself, as garrulous as my Macer, who was herself a stranger to silence.

'Never thought to break her little secret in advance though, did she? 'Course not, because you wouldn't have married her then. Would you? So, that's that. You're going to die childless, aren't you? And, she will too. Or will she? One moment – no, no she won't. She lives forever, doesn't get old, and why should she die childless, a rare beauty like her? Not when there's fellows a-plenty only too eager to help her out, bound to be. Palmer would be at the head of the queue.'

'Shut up! Shut up! Shut up!' I shouted out loud, holding my hands over my ears, horrified by myself and my own ugly, innermost thoughts.

But the seed had been planted. And, as you will appreciate, I had planted it myself.

A couple of weeks later, I drove to the life drawing class in my Rover, intending to save Laura a wet and tedious walk home. It was pouring with rain, so, blowing warm breath into my long fingers to keep the circulation flowing, I waited in the parked car by the main entrance. As always, I longed to see her. A few minutes after nine, a quartet of small groups of people emerged, separating as their feet hit the pavement and going in different directions, most with their umbrellas braced against the wind. Later, the artists' model walked out, flat-footed as a cut-price Nureyev, and recognisable despite his clothes. Amongst the students, I saw Pierre the teacher scuttle off, crossing the road and ignoring the flashing red man. Next came a solitary woman who stood in the doorway, plainly putting off the inevitable soaking until, pulling up her collar, she raced into the night.

Finally, an attractive couple arrived at the doorway, heads almost touching, deep in conversation and laughter. They were about the same height and, in some indefinable way, fitted together, seemingly at perfect ease in each other's company. The woman could only be Laura. The man I did not recognise, although I was familiar with his type: good-looking, smooth, dangerous. I watched as Laura kissed his cheek then stepped out of the studio building onto the wet pavement. Immediately, I thumped the horn hard and, with a startled look, she turned and ran back to the Rover. Seeing me, she said, 'Jock, can we give Andrew a lift? It's on our way.'

'Of course, we can,' I replied, opening the door for her from the inside and wishing I could run over Andrew there and then.

'Andrew, Andrew! Come back, quick, we can give you a lift home!' she shouted, and, all too quickly, the bastard turned around and began racing back through the puddles towards my car. He clambered into the back seat and I, surreptitiously, began inspecting him in the rear-view mirror. Too bloody handsome by half and, apparently, the same age as Laura, in so far as age can be judged by appearance.

'And what do you?' I heard myself ask him, as if I was Laura's father interrogating a possible suitor.

Traffic warden, let him be a traffic warden, I prayed. Or, better yet, given Laura's love of the gee-gees, a horse butcher.

'I'm an architect, Sir.'

Wouldn't you bloody know it, and in the use of that fake, oleaginous deferential 'Sir' my great age was being underlined.

'Jock, you can call my husband, Jock. Can't he darling?'

And I shall call him Bastard, I thought, but replied, 'Of course, he can, darling.'

The bastard's methods, for all his youth, turned out to be remarkably similar to my own. He, too, had enrolled in the University evening class on Chinese civilisation. He, too, had decided to undertake Scuba diving training at the Green Dolphin Centre. Dog-walking presented another opportunity for a chance meeting. God bless fucking Fido.

Oh, I knew what was going on, but I never confronted Laura directly. It was all too intangible, explicable as coincidence (Chinese civilisation is fascinating) or, alternatively, as a genuinely remarkable commonality of interest. Was I paranoid? Maybe, or maybe I was prescient. As I watched, conscious of what was happening but powerless to stop it, I withdrew into myself, became (I own it now, but would not have done so then), colder, more distant and, most foolishly of all, I concealed my hurt behind a carapace of pomposity and, hideous to describe, condescension.

I was, as counsel used to say in submissions, the author of my own misfortune. And in so many ways.

But one afternoon, about two months after I first had the bad luck to meet the bastard, I was in my chamber at Parliament House, surrounded by my notes, unopened textbooks and casebooks, my mind on Laura as opposed to Interim Damages, when something simple but earth-shattering hit me. I was unhappy. My strategy was not working. For all my actual, painful and prolonged abstinence from my drug, I only longed for it more. My solo state had not brought colour to my world; I missed the smiles and warmth others bestowed on my better self, and the Law remained as dry and desiccated to me as it would to a giggling child. Cold turkey had not cured this addict. It was obvious that my strategy could not work, would not work, and I could give it up. The changes wrought in me by love were irreversible, and without that love, my life was not worth living and never would be.

In short, I realised that Laura, whoever she was or whatever she was, was my life. And I was hers. She loved me; chose me. It was breathtakingly simple. At that moment, I felt a great weight fall from me; I don't know what it was, all I do know is that without it I felt light, joyous and free.

Desperate to share my epiphany with her, apologise for my foolishness and so much worse, I put on my black jacket, slung my Crombie over my shoulder and hurried along the pavements of the High Street, only to battle against the stream of the upcoming crowds who were working their way from Princes Street to the Bridges. Crossing Princes Street by the Royal Scottish

Academy, I tripped over my own over-large feet and only just managed to get out of the way of a corporation bus, the driver screaming from his window as it passed, 'Old git!'

In my state of grace, I forgave him, did not make my customary rude gesture in response, and quite unabashed by my own ineptitude, flew back to our home and managed, with uncharacteristic precision, to let myself in with my key on my first attempt. No dog greeted me. The house was in darkness and immediately I set to work.

The ruby and pearl necklace lay undisturbed below my spaghetti of high collars, and pulling it out and disentangling it, I admired my, frankly, matchless taste in jewellery. The necklace would have blinded a thieving magpie.

'Choice' was how I remembered the assistant had described it, laying it over her palm and letting the stones scintillate in the harsh artificial lighting. 'Choice indeed,' I had echoed, conscious that the discreet body in front of me had never asked for whom such finery was intended and determined, as if it mattered, to let her, and the world, know the recipient. 'My wife,' I had said proudly, 'is expecting our first child.'

At the memory, I felt a pang of pain in my heart. Our child had been born, yet I had deliberately withheld my present from my darling wife. In front of me, weeping, she had cradled its cold corpse. Now I had, finally, reconciled myself to myself, I would make up for that cruelty and all the others, a hundred times over. Bliss beckoned. We could, and would, return to our early halcyon days. If only she had it in her to forgive me.

As I was descending the stairs two at a time, I contemplated our dinner. A bottle of Veuve Clicquot was in the fridge. My own cooking skills are on the rudimentary side, but I have mastered toad in the hole with potatoes. Once, but only once, my Yorkshire pudding had passed for bought – as good as Auntie Bessie's – and I can think of no higher accolade in this day and age. Sausages had been a staple of my diet BL, so I was confident in that department. Pudding? Why, tinned peaches, of course. Another of my old standbys. I laid the table, found two newly pressed linen napkins, lit the candles and turned my thoughts as to how best I could present the necklace to my love.

After rejecting hanging it around Oliver's neck as a collar on his return (too saccharine a gesture for my taste ), I plumped for an old favourite of mine – making an oversized cracker out of newspaper and tying the ends with the pink tape that was ubiquitous in our house. So, food in the oven, I waited at the set table for my love to arrive, and tried to control my increasing excitement. I don't know why, but I have always loved giving presents. Tuesday evening was Chinese Civilisation, so all being well Laura would be back by 8 pm, a mere twenty-five minutes hence. At 8.30 pm I got up, stretched my legs and turned the oven down. Perhaps she had stopped for a quick post-lecture drink at the Apple Tree? I hoped not, but if so, it would be a 9.30 return. I got my newspaper, moved my cracker closer to her place-setting and took my seat once more.

By 10 o'clock I was beginning to feel a mixture of anxiety and anger. She must, surely, know I would be worried that something had happened to her. Could she not have found a phone box at least? Restless as a tiger, I roamed the house finding pointless things to do in one room and then in another. Should I phone round all the hospitals, just in case? Eventually, moving for moving's sake, I wandered into Laura's room, and my eye was caught by a bit of paper on the bedspread. Feeling slightly nauseous at the sight I picked it up.

> Darling Jock,
>
> I thought you had accepted me, but I am not going to stay here as you try to kill off our love. Don't look for me. I will be there when you need me most.
>
> Laura.

I cried out loud in my anguish. I needed her now! Now and forever. Andrew, fucking Andrew, would be behind this. The beautiful youth had his head in her lap and would be out to devour her. She would be with him. I took the food out of the oven, threw it in the bin, and went to bed.

# 7

The next day I was scheduled to attend to Bail Appeals first thing in the morning, but I phoned in to say I was ill, indisposed, unable to come to work.

'How long will you be off?' It was a reasonable question.

'As long as it takes . . .' I replied haughtily, then remembering I was ill, I added, 'to get better'.

The Yellow Pages contained any number of architects' firms in Edinburgh and I spent the day phoning, inquiring about drawings for a fabulously costly extension, in search of any architects named Andrew. The receptionists were, on the whole, helpful and obliging.

'A friend recommended your firm to me, suggested I speak to someone, one of your architects . . . called Andrew, I think?'

A cunning ruse, eliciting 'Sorry, no one of that name here, sir,' or, in short, 'Bingo'.

Four firms boasted an Andrew amongst their architects; one was a partner and I ranked that Andrew as least likely to be the bastard. He was, surely, too young for such seniority? Or, could he be precociously talented? No, certainly not. I put him down as fourth on my list.

I began with Andrew from Begg and Co. in Liberton. In the flesh, he turned out to be an unattractive, but possibly gifted, redhead from Northern Ireland, and despite his nice manner and genuinely inspired glazing-related ideas, I decided my extension would not be designed by him. Their most helpful receptionist, Tracy, I rewarded with a box of chocolates. Making me feel my age, the sweet child insisted on helping me on with my coat, murmuring 'Bless' as I achieved the feat of poking my arms through the sleeves. Sometimes I wonder if, in the minds of some females, there is a confusion between old men and kittens.

I managed to speak to 'Andy' from The Heaton-Hill Partnership on the phone and his cockney drawl, fortunately, brought immediate enlightenment. So 'Mr 'and' wasted no more time on him. Andrew from The Architect's Practice seemed, for a short time, likely to be my man. A rather out-of-focus photograph in The Architectural Review portrayed a good-looking fellow, with dark features reminiscent of those I had clocked at our only meeting. But hearing that he and his wife had just returned to their home-town of Warsaw, I crossed him off my list.

I had to wait a week to appraise my final Andrew, the partner in the firm of Allan and Rankin. I was ushered into his office, having given my name once more as Mr Hand, and seeing the fellow in the flesh, I am ashamed to admit, I almost fainted. Watching all the blood drain from my face, the bastard came towards me and helped me into a strange aluminium chair that appeared to be made of pipes. A cup of tea was brought in by an office girl and, having had a few sugary sips, I felt closer to my normal self. Foolishly, I had assumed my anger would make me fearless, give me all the strength I would need and allow me to confront the bastard even in his own den.

'Are you alright, Jock?' the bastard asked in a solicitous tone.

'Where is she?' I shot back.

'Sorry. Where is who?'

'Just answer my question. Laura, My wife. Where is she?'

'I have no idea. I would have thought she would be at home, with you.'

He looked at me strangely, perplexed, as if he was taking me in for the first time and needed to remember my features. A fine actor, I do concede.

'So,' I said, bluffing on, 'you won't tell me where she is?'

'No,' he said slowly, as if I was an idiot, 'I can't tell you . . . because I don't know.'

I stood up abruptly, knocking my tea onto the floor but careless of his carpets.

'Don't give me that. Tell me where she is!'

I suppose I must have raised my voice as a bulky youth came into the bastard's room and gave him an anxious glance, as if looking for instructions. He stood beside me, ready, God forbid, to restrain me; grab me. A first for me, as you may imagine. Although my dander was up, I had no idea what to do next. Too many years I had been used to people bowing and scraping to my red jersey. 'Yes, my Lord,' and 'No, my Lord,' had rendered me flabby, unfit for any confrontation in which I, personally, might be involved. Where there was equality of arms.

'I am going,' I said with as much dignity as I could

muster given that, to all appearances, I had also wet my pants. Taking care to crush the saucer beneath my feet, I went into the reception hall, and, raising my bowler in salute to the charming receptionist, I left those futuristic premises. I did not realise it until later, but, in its way, the whole thing had been a triumph. The bastard's name was Andrew Rankin, and a cursory glance at the telephone book revealed that he lived in the outer reaches of the New Town (so much for his five-star practice), in the ground-floor flat of number 35 Barony Street.

My single-minded devotion to my task over many weeks meant that a number of other matters perforce had to go by the board. I ceased leaving out cash for our rather lazy daily (Mrs Doo-sweetfannyadams) so, not unreasonably, she ceased all cleaning duties. I was sad; I liked the woman, as did Laura, although she had renamed her 'Mrs Doesweetfannyadams'. Countless telephone calls remained unanswered because I could no longer cope with the disappointment of hearing another voice at the end of the line. After one call, which I had felt sure would be her, turned out to be a double-glazing company touting for business, I yanked out the line. A few bills became overdue, and, foolishly, I no longer bothered to let the powers-that-be at Parliament House know how, or where, I was. I believe, at one stage, some kind of deputation was sent to check on my health, but I was, as was now customary, elsewhere at the time.

I did not wash. I scarcely ate, and sleep eluded me.

Day after day, I haunted the house at 35 Barony Street and, after a couple of weeks, I got lucky. There was a woman there; I saw her silhouette several times moving about in what I would hazard was a kitchen or dining room. I rapped on the door at least three times, but no one answered it. I tried the same thing every day for the next week.

Eventually, on the Saturday, a woman came in answer to a particularly loud, desperate knock, but it was not Laura. Somehow, I swallowed my disappointment.

'Good morning,' I said, raising my bowler. I was, I suppose, a little shabbier than usual as I had not shaved, my razor needing a new blade, but otherwise, I believed, I looked largely myself apart from an immoveable egg drip on my tie.

'Can I help you?'

Frankly, had I been a raving madman, the woman could not have looked more appalled. She was wearing Marigold rubber gloves and trainers, the sort of uniform favoured by Mrs Doolittle for her cleaning duties. Perhaps suspecting I might be about to assault her, she stepped backwards as if preparing herself for escape. Or was it because I stank?

'I am looking for Laura, Lady Hand. My wife?'

I had chosen my words with care. My breezy tone and the deliberate mention of the title 'Lady Hand' gave, I hoped, my inquiry an air of normality, respectability even. But, inside, my heart was battering my chest.

'Who? I'm afraid no Lady Hand stays here . . . lives here.'

'But this the home of Andrew Rankin?'

'Yes.'

'Well, is he here, by any chance?' I inquired, smiling broadly.

From my earlier, repeated reconnaissance of the house, I was fairly confident that he was not. If he was, I would, I had decided, simply persist in my attempts to extract Laura's whereabouts from him. What else was left to me? Sometimes, I think the law's gain was theatre's loss. To my ears, my question to Rankin's cleaner sounded wonderfully careless, as if I really did not give a jot either way.

'No, he's at his weekend cottage in Argyll. Not back till Sunday night.'

'Oh, yes, silly me. I should have thought of that. It's in Kilmelford isn't it? Such a lovely part of the world,' I improvised.

'Is it not Kilmartin? I'm sure it's in Kilmartin.'

'No, no. You're quite right, Kilmartin. I don't know why I get those two mixed up . . . the Kil, I suppose . . . but I always do. Many thanks for your help.'

As I walked away from his house, I noticed the woman's frightened face peeping through the half-closed door. She must have imagined that, cursing my missed opportunity, I might think better of it and spin on my toes, force my way in and molest her. Perhaps I no longer epitomised a pillar of the community in the way once I had. Regardless of that, had she but known it, an assault by a Senator of the Court of Justice (egg-stained or otherwise) might have yielded her a tabloid bonanza.

'Hands up, Lord Hand!'

'Hand-cuffed!'

'Caught red-handed!'

Perhaps, like many things, dreaming up tabloid headlines is beyond my capabilities. Actually, if I had not been so dog-tired, I might have been tempted to turn and shout 'Boo!' just to make her jump. In truth, I am not a violent man. Elaine Paige would likely throw a superior right hook. Nana Mouskouri even.

I clambered back into the Rover and drove solidly for the next four hours, going past Gleneagles, through Crianlarich, then taking the road that snakes interminably round the south side of Loch Awe. Behind the wheel, one thing and one thing alone was on my mind. I would find her, beg her forgiveness and bring her back home. Everything, everything would return to normal. I would believe her whatever she said. If she wanted a child, then I wanted that child, longed for that child. Her child, a child like her. I would retire from the Bench, kiss the law goodbye, and consider it no loss. Having tasted life with her, I had learnt that one without her was no life. She was my life.

In the local pub, chummy half-pint in hand, I discovered where Andrew, the architect from Edinburgh, lived. Those incomers, with their city-bought groceries in their Volvos and their blessed weekend cottages, eh? Bringers of death to the local shop!

Dizzy with fatigue, I found my way to his place. It was a former lodge house, situated at the end of the old carriageway between Kilmartin House and Poltalloch. Picturesque once, it now had his talentless architect's fingerprints all over it. A flat-roofed extension, PVC windows and a link block constructed of glass. Inside this poorly face-lifted monstrosity would be my treasure.

A couple of hundred yards down the road from the lodge, I sat in my car and tried to calm myself, prepare. Night was falling. I had neither eaten, nor drunk, nor slept properly for weeks and was miserable, on the edge of tears. It took a considerable and sustained effort to control myself. If they began to flow, I had little chance of stopping them. I only had to picture Laura, and they would cascade down my face, wherever I was, whatever I was doing and whoever I was with. Since she had gone, within me there seemed to be an inexhaustible well of grief. Clutching the steering wheel tight in an attempt to stop my hands trembling, I caught sight of my reflection in the mirror. My unwashed hair had acquired strange kinks, a salt and pepper stubble pocked my chin and my eyes had developed bloody rims around their sockets. A bottle of meths with a teat attached would have completed the picture. Feeling light-headed, I walked towards the lodge.

I pressed the doorbell and listened to the sound of footsteps approaching.

'You!' the bastard said as he recognised me. Facing a Bengal tiger, I doubt he would have looked more horrified.

'Where is she?' I shouted, surprising myself with my vehemence and volume.

'I told you before, I have no idea.'

'I know she's in there,' I said, looking behind him and determined to enter, find her, whatever the consequences.

'I will say it one more time. SHE IS NOT HERE!'

I moved to one side in order to get around him and as I did so, Oliver, feathery tail wagging at the sight of me, barged past him, with Fido in hot pursuit. Enraged at the bastard's lies, I shoved him as hard as I was able, but it was still only a shamefully girlie effort. I believe, in return, he must have landed a punch to my chin. Something like that. All I know is that when I woke up in hospital in Lochgilphead my jaw felt hot and swollen. Henceforth, it clicked like a castanet whenever I attempted to chew anything. A front tooth also seemed to have gone missing. Actually, I think he must have taken the opportunity to give me a bit of a doing over that night as two black eyes had also been added to my bruised features. Or, maybe, that was due to the fall.

The general consensus amongst the hospital staff, apparently not dispelled by the bastard, appeared to be that I was an evil-smelling, demented wino. 'On this occasion,' a neonate constable informed me solemnly while I lay in my hospital bed, 'you are lucky, no charges are being pressed by Mr Rankin.' Idly, I wondered what story he had told them, then grunted my heartfelt agreement in order to fulfil their expectations of my character (a single plummy word toppling from my mouth might have blown everything), keeping things simple. A day later I dressed myself in my slightly strong-smelling kit, discharged myself 'against medical advice', took a taxi to my car and drove the long road back to Edinburgh.

But I could not give up.

I filled my time by following the bastard home from his practice, hoping that I might catch a glimpse of Laura as she opened their (even now, writing that hurts) front door. For all my efforts, while I got soaked to the skin multiple times and was often torpid with cold, I never managed to see her. But where else could she be? Once or twice I shouted her name out loud in the street, hoping she would have mercy on me and show herself. But she never did. Sometimes, for a change, I patrolled the nearby public park, eyes skinned for Oliver and Fido, but all I got in return was wary glances from the young mothers clustered by the swings, suspicious, I imagine, that my unwavering gaze was actually on their little darlings rather than searching for a couple of dogs on their daily walk. God knows, I probably looked the part.

My surveillance did not go undetected however, and, a month later, I had the humiliating experience on of being served with an interim interdict, taken out by the bastard and forbidding me from going anywhere near either his practice or his home. It was signed, I noticed with a grim smile, with the languid loops so characteristic of Evan Palmer's louche hand.

A minute for imprisonment would be next, if necessary, to enforce it, and that, I knew, meant 'The Jail'. I had adjudicated on plenty of interdicts in my time but only once granted decree in a minute for imprisonment. I remember thinking, as I did so, that the fellow's behaviour was pathological (placing yet more yellow roses on the bonnet of his frightened former girlfriend's Mini despite a prohibition of going anywhere near her or her home) and that some kind of psychiatric disposal might be more humane. Anyway, after receipt of my own billet-doux, I became more furtive, increasingly cunning, but I did not desist. It was simple. All I needed to do was to talk to Laura, explain, and then everything would be alright. We would start again, afresh, time unreeling like a cotton spool.

A little less than a month later, I was peering around a corner at the bastard's house at about 7 pm when, taking me quite by surprise, he came shuffling out of it in his carpet slippers with two black bags, one slung over each shoulder. Oliver pranced along beside him. The bins were directly under a street-lamp. I could hardly believe my good fortune. As he bent to stuff one of the bags into a dustbin, I noticed that he had blood on the side of his neck. His own blood. In the agony of the moment, the realisation, I abandoned my hiding place and rushed up to him, my eyes fixed on the wound. He looked at me and, again, I saw fear in his eyes. As if I was a lunatic.

'I want to see Laura,' I demanded, telling the truth and saying the first thing that came into my head.

'Jesus Christ! You again . . .' He snatched the remaining black bag off the ground and held it in front of himself as a shield.

'Your neck, I can see blood on your neck. Laura's here, I know she's here and I want to see her, speak to her. Please, please, let me speak to her!'

'Are you mad? I've told you a hundred times, she's not here!'

'I CAN SEE YOUR NECK!' I screamed.

'So what?'

'The blood on your neck. I've seen it. I know what it means!'

'If you come any nearer, I'm getting the police. Just go away and leave me alone, won't you? Laura is not here for Christ's sake.'

'Oliver, you've got Oliver,' I said as the dog approached me, wagging his tail in recognition. I stroked him for a second. She would have stroked him.

'Yes, because she asked me to take him when she went away. You, apparently would be far "too busy" to look after him. That's what she told me. That's why I've got your bloody dog, but she's not with him.'

'Oh? And your neck? Explain that, if you can. We both know what that means!'

'What the hell are you talking about?'

'Laura's drunk your blood. Laura loves you.'

'What? Do you think she is . . . what . . . a vampire or something? Oh God, you really are a fucking lunatic . . . obsessed, deranged . . .' he said, wielding the bag now as if it was a weapon, jabbing it at me, keeping me at bay and glancing back to his door as if to calculate how long it would take him to run to safety.

'I can see your neck. I understand, I know what's happened,' I replied, trying to sound reasonable, sensible, in control. 'But all I am asking is to speak to her. Please, I just need to speak to her.'

'My neck? I cut it today on a scaffolding pole, scaffolding outside a building, just walked into it. Oh, I get it, that's where you think she bit me! Of course, it's necks they go for!'

'Let me see it then. There'll be no puncture marks, will there?' I said, darting towards him, determined to get a closer look at the wound. Thinking, I suppose, I was attacking him in some way, he struck me on the head with his rubbish bag, and, purely to protect myself from another blow, I kicked out with one of my long, ungainly limbs. My foot slammed into his knee, bruising my overlong toes, and making him emit a howl of pain. He collapsed onto the cobbles, and I heard an unpleasant cracking sound.

'Please, please, all I want to do is speak to Laura,' I begged, blood pouring down my own skull where a sharp object, maybe an open tin can, had cut through the plastic bag and into my skin. Dragging one leg as if it was broken somewhere, he limped towards his front door, muttering disgustedly in my direction, 'You fucking nutcase!'

I walked slowly back to my house, the gash on my head stinging in the bitingly cold wind. Once there, the Macallan provided some solace but not enough. I climbed into my bed, curled into a ball under the mucky, unwashed sheets and wept. I had lost her love for sure. I had seen the evidence of it and, without thought, I touched my own neck as tenderly as if it had been her sweet lips, because they had touched it. And felt comforted. Then I took too many (but, once more, not enough) of my trusty Mogadons and slept the sleep of the dead.

I was found, I later heard, by Mrs Doolittle who using her own key had come in search of her leftover work paraphernalia. I owe my continued existence upon this earth to her longing to retrieve a pair of Marigold gloves, a Magic Mop and a moss-green pinny. That good lady found me snoring and, unable to wake me, called an ambulance.

# 8

I do not want, or need, to detail exactly what happened to me thereafter. Suffice to say that the police became involved once more on my discharge from hospital, and in their kindly and cloddish way (with a nod, I suppose, from the Procurator Fiscal) they passed me on, so to speak, to those they considered 'more appropriate' to deal with me. I was considered a danger to myself and to others, and thus arrived in a locked ward within a psychiatric hospital.

My most recent assault on the bastard had, apparently, resulted in a dislocated knee-cap and a double fracture of the left femur. I myself had become closely acquainted with a stomach pump. The principal psychiatrist, Dr Marlin, declared, after many an interview, and using a rather unfashionable term, that I suffered from an 'idée fixe', which is, apparently, an external expression 'of a deeply deranged psychic individuality and probably an indicator of an incipient form of mania'.

Or so my upside-down reading revealed. No trial for me then. Had I limited myself to the 'delusion' that Laura was with the bastard, I might, stress might, have secured my release decades ago, although it wouldn't have been a foregone conclusion. It's perfectly likely that I might have remained banged up for his protection, I suppose. What ensured, and ensures, my continued stay in this institution is my description of my beloved as a vampire.

Don't get me wrong; judge or no judge, I am, like most of humanity, both willing and capable of dissembling if the need arises. For example, if my liberty depends upon it. But, there's the rub; whether she is with him or she is not, I will not deny her again. Unlike St Peter with the cock that crowed three times, I cannot do that to her more than once. He did see and know Christ (in whom numberless billions, sight unseen, believe) and I did see and know a vampire. They do exist.

She was not mad, just a being beyond my imagination. And what I can say (though nobody listens) is that if all her kind are like her, humanity would never have needed to create angels. I can give you a plethora of facts about Laura; she had eyes the colour of forget-me-nots; possessed unselfishness, sweetness and tolerance in abundance; would laugh until she choked and had enough love to redeem mankind. Oh, and she drank my blood. That being, that whole being, was my Laura, and there is one other thing. She had the power to transform me, which I did not comprehend at the time, and then I lost her and myself with her. Sometimes, the heart understands what the head cannot begin to fathom. If you will just let it.

This story is one in which for a little while, too long but only a little while, the cat thought that he was the King. 'Only accept' might, nowadays, be my motto.

Do I still think she ran off with Andrew Rankin? I cannot know, but I doubt it. He, as it turned out, was an unusually kind man and, horrified I think by his part in my precipitous downfall, came to visit me about five months after I was first committed. On reflection, maybe, one of my doctors had arranged his visit in an attempt to 'cure' me. Who knows? Oliver came with him, but did not seem to recognise me. I was still physically unwell, twitchy, largely due to my own neglect and lack of sleep. Drugged, too. I raved on at the man, unable to get that single sighting of his neck wound out of my mind and circling round and round it. Several times, in a voice which reflected his puzzlement, he tried to reassure me by telling me precisely how on the building site he had sustained the injury. Nowadays, I can think of no reason why he should have lied then. At that stage I was no danger to him, no threat to him or any life he might share with Laura. On his final visit, about five years in, he told me that he had got a postcard of the Taj Mahal from her, but he had heard nothing since. Then he confided that he thought, although he could not remember why, that she might be in Paris or, possibly, Madrid.

I know that I did not deserve her. But, and here you may believe me or not (the vast majority including my keepers do not but, in my experience, one should not read too much into that; once their psychiatric profession subscribed to the 'wandering womb' or 'animal within an animal' theories) she has been, and is, as good as her word, as I will soon explain. And me? Why did I fail her, doubt her? After all, in an attempt to appear open-minded I always gave lip service, at least, to the claim that Horatio did not know the half of it. But, as it turns out, there are indeed many more things in Heaven and Earth than this arrogant old lawyer allowed for. I was not bold enough; I could believe that she was a vampire, but not that she loved me.

If one's own mother does not love one, how could anyone else?

For those who want their pound of flesh, I have paid a price. For years, incarcerated in this place for my own safety, I have had little to do other than witness my own flesh wither and waste, my spine contract and my joints become pink and knobbly. But that is, of course, ageing, not hell; though some may think the difference more apparent than real. No, the true torture is much more subtle. To paraphrase the murderous Marlowe and blaspheme: do you imagine that I, who knew Laura and tasted the eternal joys of her love, am not in Hell in being deprived of her?

The reports of my madness are to be found in dusty filing cabinets and numerous computerised notes, but, if I am seen as enough of a 'challenge' by the newest shrink, they probe me, puzzle over me until some more colourful patient joins the club. SSRI drugs have proved ineffective, I am told, as have CBT and psychodynamic therapy. My free association tests proved insufficiently enlightening for anybody, and my dreams expose no consistent wish other than to be with her. Some believe that if I would form a strong relationship with my assigned therapist (currently Dr Spike) it would help, but, really! Our discourse almost invariably follows this sort of pattern:

'She was a vampire?' (Inquisitor looks suitably astonished.)

'Yes.'

'And you are determined to find her, track her down?' (Inquisitor needs to check that I am still a danger to myself – 'will persist in his deluded quest' – and, possibly, others.)

'To the ends of the earth. Once I am free.' (I tell the truth, and tick their box.)

Of course, it is true in principle only. Nowadays a circuit round my bed would be all I am capable of, but nobody feels the need to remind me of that fact. Perhaps they imagine I am unaware of it?

'But they don't exist, do they, no more than unicorns, dragons, fairy folk. Do they?' (Inquisitor's face sometimes expresses genuine puzzlement at my outlandish, obsessive thoughts.)

'I have never seen a dragon or a unicorn or any of the fairy folk, so I'm open-minded about them. But I have seen a vampire, have felt the blood trickle down my own neck after a vampire's bite. Placed my fingers where the teeth once were. I am "operating", as you might say, on my own first-hand experience, on information provided by my own five senses.'

'The senses are not infallible though, are they? Think of phantom limbs, Escher's drawings, the gorilla experiment where people who are tasked with counting passes in a football game fail to see a gorilla in plain view? One can't always depend upon them, can one?' (Inquisitor adopts a tone designed to reassure a five-year-old.)

'No, one can't,' I say, 'but they were good enough for doubting Thomas, though, and they're all I've got. I depended upon them until I met her, and they never let me down. Aren't they what we all depend upon, minute to minute?'

My inquisitor smiles but says nothing.

'I accept that the real world is silent,' I continue, trying to convince this one of my sanity. 'Sound, bird-song, laughter and so on are no more than air ripples detected by our ears and created by our minds. Colour does not exist there either. It's no more than different wavelengths of light reflected off different surfaces, registered by our eyes and processed by our brains. I recognise that, know all that. But you exist, I exist. I am part of your mental model of reality, you are part of mine. And we all have such models. You are no more real to me than she. In fact, if I am honest, she was much more real, more vivid . . .'

Thereafter, anything up to another hour of chatter may follow, but we always, directly or indirectly, return to my delusion and its probable causation or origin. Actually, Mummy's often in the frame, and I co-operate enthusiastically, knowing how much she relished being talked about by others; adoringly or unkindly, it was all the same to her. Incidentally, it seems the cliché about it always being your parents' fault was on the money, judging by the professionals' approach. On my way out of the man's office, I sometimes used to amuse myself by stepping on his foot, murmuring something about 'sensory malfunction' and 'faulty data'. Was it a real foot or merely a figment of my imagination?

Nowadays, when the staff overestimate my deafness, I have heard myself gigglingly referred to as 'Lord Dracula' and, once as 'Lord of the Bats'. When one of those children look closely at my wrinkled carapace and cloudy eyes, blood-sucking may seem scarcely less improbable than the idea of a creature like me, albeit in my pomp, dispensing justice to the masses. Weak as a kitten and wheelchair-bound, I no longer 'need' to be confined within a locked ward. My home has been Ward 44 for the last two years, a medical ward within the facility, but, a week ago, I was wheeled into Ward 31. It will be my last.

My heart is failing me.

Tonight, yet another new person (nurse? Auxiliary? Doctor? Who knows anymore? They all wear trainers) came on duty. At first, I took little notice of her as, in all honesty, they come and go like shadows in the night or footsteps in the street. Usually, one child simply replaces another in the tending of the failing Methuselah, and I remain as alien, as inscrutable to them as they are to me. Having closed the curtains, she came to my bedside and, feeling suddenly unbearably unloved, in need of human warmth, I opened my leaden lids and gazed up into her face, hoping for a comforting smile, no more than that. And there they were. The most beautiful eyes in this world, or any other, I might hazard. They were full of tears.

My heart leapt.

Lifting this papery old hand of mine in her perfect one, she bestowed a soft kiss upon it, saying, 'I said I would be here when you needed me.'

I nodded my head as, since late this afternoon, I have found speech all but impossible. Now I am reduced to a strange, rhythmic clicking sound, which creates a pleasing percussive counterpoint with the sound of my morphine pump. Silently, I told her that I loved her, always loved her, had never ceased loving her. I don't know what she heard, but with the greatest tenderness, she placed her lips upon my neck, and I felt a slight stinging sensation, then nothing at all. When I woke, I touched my neck, and my fingers were wet with my own blood. I gave three silent cheers. Soon, the terrors of the Birdie Invacare hoist and the inane chatter of those to whom I am no more than a job will cease.

'He lost the will to live, poor old bugger,' a pigtailed carer called Lucy opined later to her colleague.

The colleague, busily re-inflating the air cushion beneath my heels, seemed to feel no need to respond to this observation, although I believe it was made for her benefit rather than mine.

If I could get the words out, I would tell Lucy that she was wrong. It is not the will to live that I have lost; it is the will to die that I have lost. Yesterday, I felt my soul, the advance party, leave me; today, with Laura's full-blooded kiss, my body will follow. All that my carers will find when they come to minister to me at some point in the night is my cold, discarded flesh. One dead shoebill. But I know that I will be fine. You see, love does not die, and I will be with her: time without end.